T0243304

MOTHERS
and SONS

Theodor Kallifatides

TRANSLATED FROM THE SWEDISH
BY MARLAINE DELARGY

Other Press
New York

Copyright © 2007 Theodor Kallifatides
Originally published in Swedish as *Mödrar och söner* in 2007 by
Albert Bonniers Förlag, Stockholm
Translation copyright © 2024 Other Press
This translation has been published by arrangement with
Galaxia Gutenberg, S.L., Barcelona (Spain).

The cost of this translation was supported by a subsidy from
the Swedish Arts Council, gratefully acknowledged.

Production editor: Yvonne E. Cárdenas
Text designer: Patrice Sheridan
This book was set in Minion Pro & Gotham by
Alpha Design & Composition of Pittsfield, NH

1 3 5 7 9 10 8 6 4 2

Library of Congress Cataloging-in-Publication Data
Names: Kallifatides, Theodor, 1938- author. | Delargy, Marlaine, translator.
Title: Mothers and sons : a novel / Theodor Kallifatides ; translated from the
Swedish by Marlaine Delargy.
Other titles: Mödrar och söner. English
Description: New York : Other Press, 2024.
Identifiers: LCCN 2024010673 (print) | LCCN 2024010674 (ebook) |
ISBN 9781635423006 (paperback) | ISBN 9781635423013 (ebook)
Subjects: LCSH: Kallifatides, Theodor, 1938-—Fiction. | Mothers and sons—
Fiction. | LCGFT: Autobiographical fiction. | Novels.
Classification: LCC PT9876.21.A45 M6413 2024 (print) |
LCC PT9876.21.A45 (ebook) | DDC 839.73/74—dc23/eng/20240312
LC record available at https://lccn.loc.gov/2024010673
LC ebook record available at https://lccn.loc.gov/2024010674

MOTHERS *and* SONS

THE STARTING POINT

WHEN I WAS LITTLE I thought I would die before my mother, according to the principle that the tree outlives its fruit.

As time went by I came to understand the correct, or at least natural order of things, which gave me a new problem: How could I inflict on her the pain my death would bring? This realization made me careful and moderate, even as a child. My games were never particularly reckless, and I mostly stayed pretty close to her, which is something she occasionally reminds me of when I call her on Saturdays.

She lives in Athens. I have lived in Stockholm for the past forty-two years.

These are almost ritualistic phone calls. They take place preferably in the morning, soon after she gets up and is sitting with her cup of coffee on her lap. That's how she holds her cup, resting on her stomach. She takes hesitant little sips, because she is afraid that the coffee won't be sweet enough. The absolute minimum is three spoonfuls of sugar.

"Hi Mom, it's me," I say when she picks up.

If she's in a good mood, she answers with a little poem. If she isn't in a good mood, she soon will be.

> *Good morning my son in a foreign land*
> *who sometimes calls*
> *and brings joy to his mother*
> *who is older than he thinks.*

You might imagine it's the same poem every time, but it isn't. Even at the age of ninety-two she has the ability to play with language. Then it comes: "You hardly left my side when you were a little boy, and yet you traveled so far away."

This is not an accusation but rather a mystery she is unable to solve. I don't have an answer either. I left my country, that's true, but what was it I actually wanted to leave behind?

We don't discuss the matter any further. It is what it is. My mother has always known that everything is what it is. It's not just part of her backbone, it *is* her backbone, this stoical attitude to life that she has inherited, the gift of being able to let the small elements of joy defeat the great sorrows. The warm coffee cup resting on her stomach is an atomic bomb of joy, especially with *four* spoonfuls of sugar.

Therefore, because we both know that it is what it is, we talk about other things.

THIS YEAR I TURNED sixty-eight, and my mother ninety-two.

"I wasn't the main cause of the First World War, but I was born in the year it began," she sometimes says with the playful irony that has always prevented her emotions from overwhelming her.

We have both grown old and it is becoming increasingly urgent for me to do what I have wanted to do for a long time: to write about her.

I didn't want to write about her while she was still alive, but now it seems as if I have no choice. Death is approaching for both of us. We cannot know whose death is taking the longest strides.

I have to write about her, and assume that she will read what I write. It will probably turn out to be a completely different book from the one I had imagined. Right now I don't know what kind of book it will be.

When my father died, I wrote a book about him. When his remains were dug up some years later because there was a shortage of space in the churchyard, I wrote about him again.

It was difficult, but not too difficult. My father was dead. His life was over. The book about him was already written, so to speak.

But my mother is still alive.

I AM ABOUT TO visit her in Athens. This time I will take my notebook with me. I have prepared a number of questions for her. I feel nervous, and I don't really like it. I don't want to treat my mother as material for a book. The son in me just wants to be with her like before, restfully and with no particular purpose in mind. To sit with her on the balcony, to listen to her as she complains about the government or the neighbor, to ask her to "read" the coffee grounds in our cups.

The author in me wants something else. I will be noting every gesture she makes, every word she says. How will this affect me? How will it affect her, when she realizes what I am doing?

There is no way of knowing. I remember when an eminent artist was going to paint a portrait of me. I was flattered and readily agreed, only to discover after a couple of sittings that I had stopped being myself and was behaving like someone else. The artist's eye had colonized me and made me act like a deferential subject. If I could guess what that eye demanded of me, then I would make sure I did exactly that. Posing means looking at oneself through the other person's eyes. That is what successful models do: They intuitively know what the photographer wants to see, and they deliver it.

I don't want to force my mother to pose for me.

How can I avoid it?

Is it even possible?

There is another problem.

How am I going to keep the writing demon, who is determined to take over, in check? The demon who wants to embroider, joke, beautify or uglify, exaggerate, turn a hen into a pheasant and a pheasant into a hen?

Few, if any other professionals, have such difficulty in sticking to reality. Talented writers are often terrible journalists. Which doesn't mean that talented journalists are terrible writers.

Why am I worrying so much?

Then I suddenly realize what the real issue is: I will be able to continue writing only as long as my mother is alive. Once she is gone there will not be one single line more. I think.

So the question remains: How far had I moved away from her side, even though I traveled so far?

I ONCE HAD A dear friend, now dead, who told me that Dostoyevsky had made her into a human being and Chekhov had made her into a woman.

I feel the urge to make a travesty of her words.

My father made me into a human being, but it is my mother who made me an author.

In my father's world there was work, duty, perseverance, saving your tears until all the smiles had run out.

In my mother's world, things were different. There was closeness and the nervous anxiety that goes with it; there was unpredictability, vulnerability, and the need for everything to be okay again at the end of the day. Tears and smiles were not polar opposites but a prerequisite of each other. A rapid statistical calculation tells me that my mother cried the most when she laughed the most. And above all, memory existed in her world.

Moving on was my father's lodestar.

My mother prefers to go backward.

It is from her that I have acquired my desire to tell stories. The desire that is in a way a wish for everything to be okay again, to reach the right place, to find a meaning and a context.

All of this can be expressed more succinctly.

For my father, life was tomorrow.

For my mother, life is yesterday.

Their marriage was an unlikely union.

How likely was it that a boy born in 1890 in Trebizond by the Black Sea in a poor district outside the walls would marry a girl born in 1914, twenty-four years later, in an insignificant village in the southern Peloponnese? If you look at the map, you will understand. Extremely unlikely. And yet they married and lived together for almost fifty-four years.

ALL THIS IS SO long ago that I need to start from the beginning. As is appropriate, I will start with the dead. With my father.

When he was alive he rarely talked about his life. He was a taciturn man and the past, as I have already said, was a closed chapter as far as he was concerned. And yet he remembered everything with remarkable clarity.

This became evident when at the age of eighty-two he wrote a lengthy piece about his life, not for publication but for me. The first sentence says: "My beloved Theodor wants me to write about the origin of our family, the Kallifatides family."

In other words, he wouldn't have done it if I hadn't asked him.

It is through this text that I know what I know about him and how he met my mother.

Recently, in fact on one of the very first spring days when the heart—or my heart, at least—is filled with inexplicable and inaccessible melancholy, I sat down with his text.

It was written purely for my sake. So I have to ask myself: Would it be right for me to keep it hidden from others?

No, it would not. It is a testimony from different times. It is not a story, a novel, or an essay. It is simply a life, that of my grandchildren's great-grandfather.

So while I am at the airport in Copenhagen waiting for the plane to Athens, I take out a pen and paper and begin to translate the text for their sake. They are too young to ask me to do this, and by the time they are grown-up enough to ask, I will probably not be available.

MY FATHER'S STORY

MY FATHER BEGINS HIS story by writing the wrong date.

"Athens, March 22, 1922," it says, but it was 1972. It is a significant error: 1922 was the year in which his life took a new direction, which will become clear later on. It is as if we remember different things, we and our memory.

And so the text continues.

My beloved Theodor wants me to write about the origin of our family, the Kallifatides family.

I am now eighty-two years old, and no one will be offended if I simply write what I remember.

My grandfather's name was Giannis Kalafatidis or Kalafatoglou or just Kalafat. One of his grandchildren, who was called Lambos, didn't think that sounded right. So he changed it to Kallifatidis with a double *l*.

It is likely that one of our forefathers repaired boats. The word for this is *kalafat*, and involves filling various holes with tar and hemp. Maybe that is where our family name comes from.

My grandfather was born in a village in the province of Gemoura in the district of Trebizond.

The village was called Little Samarouxa, some twelve miles from Trebizond and ten miles from the west coast of the Black Sea. It might have gotten its name from the self-seeding strawberries that grow there in large amounts.

However, Gemoura was principally known for exporting hazelnuts. Almost every variety of fruit tree grew there, and some only there and nowhere else.

In ancient times Gemoura was the site of the famous gardens established by Aeëtes, the father of Medea and the king of Colchis, as it was known back then. When I was a boy there was still a village called Colcha, where you could see remains and ruins from long, long ago.

At this point I have to set my father's text aside, reluctantly. I need to breathe. His words about Medea and those ancient, beautiful gardens move me so deeply. It is always heartrending when you are unexpectedly faced with the memories of humanity.

A while ago I got into conversation with a middle-aged guy at the gym. He was a former Syrian fighter pilot who had lived in Sweden for many years. I didn't know how he had ended up here, whether he was a hero or a deserter, which of course doesn't preclude the possibility that he was a hero for that very reason. It turned out that he was thinking about heroes. We were discussing the value of various exercises when he pointed to the pull-up bar.

"That's the best. That's how Achilles trained," he said, as if he were referring to someone who had just left.

I was almost in tears. With those few words he had swung back in time more than twenty-eight hundred years. The gym in which we were standing expanded, it became an open-air arena beneath a blue sky in a different country.

The past is all we have.

That is why I am so gripped by my father's words about Medea and her father. I close my eyes and try to picture Medea as a young dark-haired princess, running around in her father's beautiful gardens. She has not yet met Jason, the man who will steal the Golden Fleece, and who also took the opportunity to steal her heart and made her commit dreadful atrocities: dismembering her brother's body in order to save her lover, and much later slaughtering her own children to take revenge on him when he left her.

How can I explain to my grandchildren the fragile thread that bound their great-grandfather to his world when they have no idea who Medea or Jason were, when they have never heard of the Golden Fleece or the Argonauts?

I must make sure they learn. That is what I would like to leave behind, more than anything: the scent of a human life, the scent that, although it is not sharp, cuts through time like a perfectly honed knife through a ripe apple.

I look around me as I sit there at the airport in Copenhagen, waiting for my connecting flight to Athens. I recognize some of my fellow passengers. Men and women who, like me, are growing old in a different country, and are once again on their way to Greece in the hope of rediscovering...what?

Year after year they fly back and forth, incapable of remaining in the new or returning to the old. I am one of them.

I have to order a beer from the sour-faced Danish waiter in order to stop myself from becoming too pompous. After all, it is possible to live a good life without knowing about Medea, or so they say, and I agree with that, although deep down I doubt it.

How can you live a full life without the shadow of humanity behind your back?

"Can you live without knowing about Medea and Jason?" I ask the waiter when he brings my beer.

He is not surprised. He doesn't look at me as if I am crazy. No doubt he has been asked many strange questions over the years.

"I don't know, but a sandwich always helps," he replies eventually.

My mother might have said the very same thing.

It is time to return to my father, who continued to write about the riches of the Black Sea, about the enormous quantities of fish that were exported as anchovies all over Europe. My father had been a teacher, and he had no intention of letting an opportunity to educate pass by. He went on to say that the ancient Greeks desired the fertile earth and the fish-rich sea so strongly that they founded many colonies there, including the town where he was born. Goods from the Black Sea or the region known as Pontus were famed in ancient times and commanded a higher price than the same goods from other regions. After this foray into golden times, but times that were long gone, he returned to his family and the situation in which they found themselves, which was anything but golden.

I never knew my grandfather. He was dead when I was born. My grandmother was also dead. They had five sons and one daughter. Three of the boys emigrated to Russia. The tsar gave immigrants rough tracts of forest. With hard work, the forest was transformed into fertile ground. Several immigrants made considerable fortunes, primarily cultivating corn and tobacco. Over time they also began to breed animals, especially large animals like cows, oxen, and horses, but also chickens for their own use. However, they were not permitted to sell their property in order to return to their homeland. When the Communists came to power in 1917, many immigrants went over to their side and became Russian citizens. Others preferred to leave everything they had created through their hard work, and to go back home. Some arrived in Greece as refugees. Of my grandfather's three sons, only one returned.

Once again I am forced to set aside my father's text, and the sour-faced Danish waiter looks worried. What weird question am I going to ask him now?

But I am not going to ask him anything. I am thinking about the tsar's immigration policy. Is it possible to learn from it?

It is also worth considering the fanaticism of the Bolsheviks—either with us or against us. Aren't we following the same track?

Then there is the matter of coming to terms with the realization that I might have relatives in modern-day Russia. Many years ago a Finnish colleague told me that he had seen my family name in one of Solzhenitsyn's books, probably *Cancer Ward*. I made an attempt to read it, but my days of reading a six-hundred-page novel were definitely gone. I never found what I was looking for, which was perhaps just as well. Because if there was someone in that book, he was certainly dead.

The thought makes me smile sadly at the Danish waiter, and I signal that I would like another drink. Then I continue reading.

Only two of my grandfather's six children spent their entire lives in the village of Samarouxa. They died there, they were buried there, and that is where their bones remained, in St. George's churchyard with no grave lantern and no incense, wholly dependent on the goodwill of our Turkish neighbors.

Only these two, my uncle Konstantis and my father, Giorgios, stayed in the village and built families of their own. They worked in agriculture, forestry, and the breeding of small animals.

The women baked the family's bread in the ovens they had constructed themselves. They milked the cows and made yogurt, butter, and cheese. They sowed hemp and flax, which they then used to make everything from rope to clothes. They sheared the sheep and used the wool to make fabric for the men's winter clothing. They also made earthenware with their own hands—pans, plates, carafes, containers for oil and wine. They let the vessels dry out in the shade for a few days, then they lit a big bonfire to fire them. When they removed the items they treated the insides with a mixture of water and flour while they were still very hot. This gave the pots a wonderful sheen, and made them much less porous. It was challenging work, and everyone helped.

Life was primitive and hard in the villages in Turkey back then. There was no money—and no supplies either. You had to travel to Trebizond, the main center of the area. At the time it had fifty thousand inhabitants. Greeks and Turks lived together in harmony. Turkey was still an empire, and the sultan was Abdülhamid. There was peace and religious freedom.

The Greeks had their churches and schools, which functioned perfectly well with no involvement from the authorities.

In every Greek community there were elementary schools with six or seven classes, which were funded by the community.

These schools taught Greek language and history, without any interference from the authorities. This lasted until the Young Turk Revolution in 1908–1909. They declared a new constitution and the sultan lost all his power. That was the beginning of the purging of the Greeks from Turkey.

It wasn't only the Greeks who were persecuted. Armenians and Jews suffered just as much. It has taken almost a century for the truth to become known.

There is a great deal that humanity has not talked about.

How can we sleep so well at night?

By now I have finished my second beer, so this time I order a double espresso, ignoring my godfather's advice: "Never order a double espresso. The only thing that's doubled is the water."

He was a restaurant owner in New York, so he ought to know.

I'm not joking. My godfather used to own a restaurant in Manhattan.

I lived with him in New York for a month. He showed me pictures of the place he once owned, posing with Michael, the former king of Romania. When I was there he had switched horses and become a florist. His store was high up on York Avenue, a pretty rowdy area. One evening when the two of us were sitting quietly, three young men stormed in—one Black and two Latino. They smelled of trouble from a mile off. My godfather remained calm. He picked up the baseball bat he kept under the counter, and asked them politely, "What do you want? Money or trouble?"

There was something in his voice that made those three young men look at one another and make one of the most sensible decisions in their lives. They turned around and disappeared.

My whole body was shaking, but my godfather laughed.

"I eat their sort for breakfast," he said.

Which was good, because he didn't eat anything else for breakfast. I have never seen a person work so hard. He got up at four o'clock in the morning to collect the flowers from the airport, where they arrived on big planes from Florida. By six he was back in the store, sorting out the newly purchased blooms and plants. He opened at seven and didn't close until ten o'clock at night. Then he went to a nearby trattoria and ate a steak. Nothing else, exactly the same thing all week. He also drank coffee. Lots of coffee. At eleven o'clock he fell into bed.

He did that for twenty years, until he decided to move back to the village as a well-to-do emigrant and an American pensioner. He bought a pretty property, made himself a cup of coffee, and it was there on the terrace that the viper struck, while my godfather was enjoying the view of the bare mountains in the distance and the blue sea close by.

He was lucky to survive. That's how it is. For emigrants, life is always somewhere else, but the snakes lie in wait everywhere. Many members of my family have dreamed the immigrants' dream, and there are many who still have that dream.

I have relatives all over Europe, in Asia, Australia, America, and Canada. We are spread right across the globe. I could print a separate little run of my books for my relatives. With this cheering thought it is time to return to my father's text.

He wrote that his uncle was murdered by the Turks in 1922. His uncle's family dispersed, some members leaving no trace behind. He went on:

My father was my grandfather's fourth son. His name was Giorgios, or Giorikas in the local dialect. He was illiterate, as were his siblings. He was blond-haired, blue-eyed, and very tall—over six feet. He never learned a craft, but he was a good agricultural worker and a fanatical hunter.

My mother was slightly darker skinned, like wheat grain, and of medium height. Her name was Eleni. Her family came from inland, where the men worked in the mines at Argyroupolis, known in ancient times. The name literally means Silver Town. The silver mining eventually ceased, and the family moved to the Black Sea coast.

I was born in Trebizond in the district of Exoticha in 1890.

I had read this text several times before, and yet I had missed two important details. First, my father didn't know his date of birth. The year might have been 1890, or it might not. He had no idea of the month, or the day of the month. We never celebrated his birthday, because we didn't know when it was.

Second, his place of birth. The district of "Exoticha"— outside the walls. What does that mean? Simply that the family was very poor. It was the sick and the poor who lived outside the walls. Hence his lifelong struggle, a struggle I inherited. It would become the most important aspect of my adult life as an emigrant—the battle to get inside the walls.

People who are born inside the walls can never understand this. How could they? To them the walls offer protection, to the rest of us they are a barrier.

Imagine if we inherit not only our parents' genes but also the defining structures of their lives, like for example being born inside or outside the walls. In the seventies there was much talk of the class journey. The whole of Sweden moved up a step. Laborers became engineers, nurses became doctors, janitors became office managers in the national or local government hierarchy, farmhands became politicians, and so on. It was beautiful, but isn't it also a part of Sweden's problem? The fact that office managers also have to act as janitors sometimes, and that politicians easily revert to being farmhands?

What can we learn from this?

That society changes faster than the people within it.

It is a sobering thought, so I return to my origins.

My father knocked on doors and sold vegetables. He didn't earn very much. When I was eight months old my mother had to leave me with her mother so that she could work as a wet nurse for the Russian consul, who had a baby boy the same age as me. His wife didn't have enough milk, my mother had more than I needed. She divided her days between the consulate and home. After a while she would take me with her to the consulate, where little Kolja and I would share her. Her pay was two Turkish gold pounds. In those days it was quite common to work as a wet nurse.

Many new mothers from wealthy families either suffered from a shortage of milk or decided to employ a wet nurse for other reasons, after rigorous medical checks.

We stayed at the consulate for five years, which improved our financial situation. In the third year my father was taken on as the consulate's general factotum. He wore a uniform and carried a service weapon, and he accompanied the consul everywhere, particularly on hunting expeditions.

At the consulate we lived like kings. Kolja and I played all day. My mother often took us for long walks. This life was unforgettable, even though I was only a five-year-old child.

Sadly, everything came to an abrupt end. The consul was recalled to Russia, and his successor didn't require the services of my parents. And so in March 1896 we returned to our village of Samarouxa, and to poverty.

How could he remember all those details?

Perhaps because he too knew that the past is all we have.

IT IS TIME TO head for the gate, but I don't stand up immediately. I suddenly feel as if it isn't at all necessary. I could sit here at the airport for a while longer, read my father's words in the secure knowledge that I have a journey ahead of me, rather than behind me.

Reason triumphs eventually. I walk slowly toward the gate, where a surprise awaits me. An imposing elderly lady with gray hair, peppercorn-black eyes, and a black walking stick makes a beeline for me with almost fearsome determination. People step aside to let her pass, as if they sense that this is going to be entertaining.

She stops in front of me, at walking-stick length.

"Are you the one who writes books?" she demands, loudly enough for the entire line to hear. I am uneasy to say the least.

"It might be a little too generous to call them books," I reply, attempting to appease her without knowing why.

"You ought to be ashamed of yourself. How can you slander your country like that? Are you a Greek or a Bulgar?"

The question makes me recoil, not only literally but also mentally. I was seven years old again in Molai, the village where I was born. There were lots of Greeks, but also the odd person who was regarded as a Bulgar, including my father and his offspring. This was in 1945, the German army was retreating. The vacuum they left behind was filled by right- and left-wing groups fighting each other and taking turns terrorizing the rural communities. Being a Bulgar was tantamount to high treason, it meant betraying one's fellow citizens, selling out one's country, and plenty more along those lines. Being a Bulgar meant allying oneself with the Communist swine, spitting on Jesus who was crucified for our sake, betraying the Greek way of thinking and living.

The advantage of being seven years old is that you haven't had a great deal of time to fit in much betrayal. However, that didn't keep me from being beaten up by a gang of older boys.

Standing there in front of the elderly lady, I know it is important not to give the wrong answer, and above all not to dismiss the question, because this is often regarded as the first step toward a confession. Several of the Greek travelers come closer, making me think of some kind of temporary people's tribunal.

"I have never slandered my country. I simply tell it like it is."

"Why can't you answer like a man?" someone says.

"And why have you popped up like a fart?" asks someone else who is clearly an advocate of free speech.

"Are you calling me a fart? Come over here and say that!"

I step in. "Why are you arguing? I'm the one with the problem."

The stern lady speaks up again. "You're the one who's making us argue. You divide the Greeks and fool those boneheaded Swedes. People ask me if Greeks sleep with their goats or hit their wives and kids morning, noon, and night. I'll soon be too scared to go out. The whole of Västervik is laughing at me. My whore of a daughter-in-law left my son because he gave her a slap when she made out with another guy right in front of him. You've made us a laughingstock. I spit on the ground where you stand."

At which point she aims a virtual gob of spit at my feet.

An old nightmare has kicked in. I have always dreaded the day when a self-righteous Greek takes me to task, not because of what is happening but because I talk about it.

I don't know what to say or do, but then I have an idea.

"I wonder if you've read my books?"

She doesn't miss a beat. "Such a thing would never occur to me," she snaps, walking back to her seat.

I sit down too. The people around me lose interest. The woman might have been wrong, but she had asked an important question: Can you be an author without betraying someone or something?

Was I about to betray my mother?

At that moment there was no help to be had, except possibly from the man who has always helped me.

I began to read my father's words again.

After a while my sister Elisavet was born—or Lisaf in the Black Sea dialect. Our parents both worked, and the two of us were alone all day. By the time they came home in the evening they were almost too exhausted to eat.

There were no olive trees in Samarouxa, because the village was a long way from the sea and located at quite a high altitude. When it was time to harvest the olives my parents traveled to villages six or seven hours away. They were paid in kind, that is to say in olive oil. It was impossible for them to get home each night, so during October and November we children were left by ourselves.

This was sheer torture for me and Lisaf because we were the oldest and had to take care of our siblings. We cooked, we washed, we looked after the little ones—in short, we did everything that needed doing.

This, especially for me, was pure slavery, because I also had to go to school and never had time to do my homework.

My parents had five children. I got through my seven years of elementary school with great difficulty and hardship, and in September 1904 I was enrolled at the high school in Trebizond. Its official name was Trebizond Greek High School, and it was an attractive building that had been erected on the ruins of a former school. The institution had an impressive history: It was founded in 1682 by the Greek scholar Sevastos Kyminitis. This original school kept Greek education and the Greek language alive for Greeks by the Black Sea for close on two centuries.

My studies were very challenging for me and a burden to my parents, because they had to pay for my accommodation in the town. This was very hard, given their small income. I was fourteen years old, living alone and having to take care of myself as well as studying, without access to the necessary books. So I had to stay behind at the end of the day and borrow books from my classmates or from the school library.

Having gotten so far, I have to set aside my father's text because it is time to board the plane. With some anxiety—what if I end up sitting next to the sanctimonious lady?—I search for my seat. My neighbor turns out to be a Swedish woman who is an archaeologist, working on a dig somewhere in Greece.

"I love Greece," she says.

"Just as well," I reply, demonstratively getting out my earplugs. I have no desire to hear the reasons why she loves Greece. The important thing at this moment is whether I have any reason to do the same.

I was brought up to love Greece, which in principle meant I had been taught to love and obey its masters: the king—there was one when I was young—and the church. I rebelled against both, and eventually left my country. A few people remained. Over time these people became fewer. Now I am on my way to see the only two who are left: my mother and my brother.

There is, however, a difference between these two. My brother is The Greek. Easily offended, greedy for life's pleasures, misunderstood, constantly opposed to everything, the man who dreamed of affixing windshield wipers to his TV so that he could spit at the screen when he was watching football. Quick-witted, quick to like someone and equally quick to do the opposite. Every time I spoke about Greeks, I thought about my brother. But he isn't Greece. That is my mother. The day my mother is gone, then Greece will be gone too.

I've said this before, but suddenly it seems to me that it was an oversimplification. My mother might well be Greece, but is she the whole of my Greece?

I close my eyes and think back. I remember the smell of the ground after rain in my village, and the long afternoons with my friend Kostas, who is dead now, when we talked about our love for the same girl. The memory of the day I tried out for the Panathinaikos F.C. junior team is as vivid as if it were yesterday, not to mention my first kiss. Her lips tasted of oranges. I remember a thousand things and people and events. None of these will disappear when my mother is gone.

No one's death is definitive. Maybe she will give me the gift of a new country when she is gone. After all, that was what my father had done. The story of his life gave me another Greece, namely the Greek settlements by the Black Sea, which had been there since seven hundred years before Christ, and which had survived the Persians and the Romans and the Russians and the Turks.

The Black Sea. The ancient Greeks called it "the inhospitable," but because they were not entirely devoid of humor, they sometimes spoke of "the hospitable." That is the name that can still be found on Greek maps, but all others have "the Black Sea," yet another piece of evidence to prove that my brother is right: The Greeks are misunderstood.

I go back to my father's words.

I lived on the ground floor in a room with a small window. My furniture consisted of a table riddled with woodworm, a wicker chair, a portable stove to keep me warm, and a size-five kerosene lamp, my only source of light. My bed was an old wooden chest. My usual menu was beans or potatoes with olive oil or kavourna—goat meat that is first fried then allowed to dry. My mother walked from the village once a week, bringing bread, olive oil, and sometimes butter that she had made herself, along with charcoal that my father produced in the forest. Two years passed in this way.

In the third and fourth years, my maternal uncle gave me a room in his home. He was a multitalented man. He ran a café, he was a barber, he extracted teeth, and he also practiced bloodletting using a special glass cup. Bloodletting was very common in Turkey; it was carried out by barbers, usually during the month of May. A surface incision is made in the arm, then the cup is applied. The procedure was regarded as good for a person's general health, and also for colds and any kind of pain.

I hadn't seen this method of bloodletting. The practitioner in my village used leeches, which was no fun at all. However, cupping was used, particularly for colds. My maternal grandmother had once done it to me.

First of all she washed my upper body with pure spirit. Then my mother lit a small torch, which my grandmother used to warm the glasses. She pressed them against my back, then my chest. I watched as my skin rose up and big beads of sweat sprang forth. I could almost literally see the cold leaving my body.

I didn't need to undergo bloodletting, because I had frequent nosebleeds. My nose would start to bleed unexpectedly, as I was sitting there peacefully. It was some kind of overflow, which was what my great-grandmother used to say.

"It's nothing, It's just the bad blood coming out."

"The bad blood." Terrifying. I had two kinds of blood: a good kind that didn't pour out, and a bad one that did.

"Are they different colors?" I asked my great-grandmother.

"How stupid can you be?" she replied.

She had no time for her great-grandchildren. She called me "Big Cock." I was three years old.

It suddenly strikes me that I can no longer recall her name, and I make a note to ask my mother.

The captain informs us that we have reached a cruising altitude of thirty thousand feet.

This is an excellent opportunity to travel almost a hundred years back in time.

Unfortunately my maternal uncle lived alone. His family had remained in the village. The combined café and barbershop were located on the most central street in Trebizond. He worked all day, every day and came home only to sleep.

I didn't have to pay rent, and each morning I stopped in at the café for a cup of tea, a slice of bread, and some olives. It was on the way to school, which made things easier. In return I worked there on Sundays, and any other day when the school was closed.

And so the years passed. I completed my studies in 1908. I was the first person from my village to do so, and it was regarded as a major achievement. My relatives and neighbors celebrated with song, lute music, dancing, and lots of wine. The lute, with three silk strings, was played by an older guy who was renowned in the area. My father wept with joy and slaughtered one of his two calves. Even our Turkish neighbor and his family joined in with the party.

I paused at that point, because it struck me how different the situation had been when I graduated from high school in 1956. I was eighteen years old, filled with anxiety and restlessness, busy searching for something as anachronistic as the meaning of life. My girlfriend had left me for an ape who walked with his legs wide apart and spat between his teeth. Sports no longer appealed to me. "Only a healthy love life can save a young person from sport," according to Oscar Wilde. In my case, the reverse was true. I was saved by my sorrow over a lost love. Instead of going home with my final grades, I boarded a train heading north, intending to travel to the holy mountain of Athos and become a monk. I didn't make it. I ran out of money in Thessaloniki in a way that suggested the life of a monk was perhaps not suitable for me. I visited a bar, where a number of girls were employed to attract the male clientele. You had to buy them a bottle of wine in order to have any chance of arousing their interest.

I spent all my money on one of them, a dark-haired beauty whose slight squint made her seem wise and all-seeing. She let me weep in her arms while she ordered one bottle after another. I had only just enough to cover the bill, at which point she lost all interest in me. Alone, tired, and broke I had no choice but to return home.

Some years later I boarded a northbound train again. With various stopovers, it took me all the way to Sweden and Stockholm. This time I didn't go back.

At the age of eighteen, my father had other concerns.

And now I had to work. There was no way the family could afford to let me carry on studying.

In those days a high-school education was regarded as sufficient to become a teacher. There were even teachers who had completed only elementary school.

In September 1908 I was employed as a teacher in the village of Strouké. The following year I moved to a bigger village, Kartséa, where I stayed for five years. I was satisfied with my profession and worked very conscientiously.

I always got the best reports from the school inspectors—but I was very tired. I had to run my household alone, cooking my meals and taking care of my clothes. I also had to watch my spending. I set most of my salary aside so that I could help my parents. Fortunately, I didn't need to pay rent. The school provided a room with a kitchen. I would prepare food for several days in advance. I got wood from my pupils' parents. There was no grocery store in the village, but the kind and hospitable villagers gave me everything I needed: oil, eggs, bread, chickens, potatoes, beans, and so on. In this way I managed to save ten Turkish pounds in my first year, and we were able to repair the leaking roof at home. My parents had tears in their eyes.

I also have tears in my eyes, cruising at thirty thousand feet. Why is happiness always mingled with tears for the Greeks? My mother has tears in her eyes when I arrive and when we say goodbye. She has tears in her eyes when she sees my picture in a newspaper, or when she is telling a funny story. The gratitude for the chance to be happy is always greater than the happiness itself. Her tears of joy spring from the well of humility. "Who am I to be given the chance to feel so happy?" That is the question these tears pose, and we all have reason to ask it.

The archaeologist sitting beside me notices that I am wiping my eyes, and anxiously inquires if I am okay.

"I'm fine. I'm just kind of happy," I reply, and return to my father's narrative.

The school in the village of Kartséa had between seventy and eighty pupils, divided into six classes. I was the only teacher and had a great deal to do. I worked from dawn to dusk, and I still couldn't get everything done. I chose a good student from the oldest class and asked him to look after the youngest children, after spending several days preparing him.

Five years passed in this way, and in September 1913 I moved to the school in Oinoe, a coastal town to the east of Trebizond.

It was the first time I had traveled so far from my home and my parents.

We left Trebizond, a colleague and I, aboard a small sailing ship with a Muslim skipper and crew.

The voyage took two days. Fortunately we had good weather.

Crossing the Black Sea always holds surprises. There are often violent storms. The seafarers of the ancient world changed its name from the inhospitable to the hospitable in order to appease it.

(And I thought, as I wrote earlier, that it was evidence of their sense of humor.)

At that time Oinoe had nine thousand inhabitants: Turks, Greeks, Armenians, Jews, and a small number of Europeans. The Greek community was made up of four thousand Orthodox Christians, and it ran excellent schools. I started work at one of them; there were eight teachers.

I was very happy with my job and my salary. Unfortunately, toward the end of the year I was forced to move on. For what reason? The First World War broke out, and Turkey participated on the side of the Central Powers. The war lasted from 1914 until 1918. Almost the entire world was split into two camps: England, France, Italy, Russia, Japan, North America, Greece, and Serbia on one side, and Germany, Turkey, Austria, and Bulgaria on the other.

The Turks were angered by the prosperity of the Greek community. The odd Greek was murdered. There were rumors that the Greeks would be forcibly relocated to the interior of the country. The Christians became increasingly afraid.

During this period I happened to receive a letter from one of my mother's sisters, who lived in Constantinople. She wrote that I was welcome to go and stay with her. I didn't waste any time. I gave my notice despite the principal and my colleagues pleading with me to stay.

No passenger ferries visited the harbor at Oinoe. I had to take a carriage to Sampson, then travel by boat to Constantinople. I made an arrangement with a Turkish carriage driver, and very early on August 6, 1914, I left Oinoe. The heat was unbearable.

We drove all day, and in the evening we reached the river Thermidon, where according to mythology the realm of the Amazons lay. It was low water, and we managed to drive across. We spent the night at a *chani* (a kind of simple hostel). The following day we set off very early once again, and arrived in Sampson toward dusk. I spent the night with a Greek family.

What family? He doesn't say. Presumably he didn't know them, but that's how the world worked once upon a time. You knocked on a door and asked if there was room for you to sleep. There usually was.

So much has been told and written about the lone traveler who knocks on a door. The girls in the household are curious and excited, the parents try discreetly to find out as much as possible about the guest. Sometimes there is a daughter who is no longer quite so young and hasn't yet managed to find a husband. It often ends with a wedding.

I had one foot in this warm world, where every door was open. It was the poor world, where people depended on one another in a tangible way.

From my childhood I remember the people of my village gathering in the square to wait for the bus from the capital. There was always someone among the passengers who had nowhere to go, and the villagers competed with one another to offer this person a roof over his or her head.

This wasn't simply a good deed but also something that enhanced the status of the host. Everyone respected the individual who kept his door open. When the traveler had moved on, the villagers sought out the host to hear the stories the visitor had had to tell. Every visitor left behind a wealth of unfamiliar towns and countries, the heart of the village expanded, and it became a little easier to breathe and to dream.

The following day the villagers would be back in the square, waiting for the bus.

I am suddenly overcome with such a powerful longing for that village, for those afternoons in the square, that I think my heart is going to stop. I can't breathe.

Then again, it could be an attack of nicotine withdrawal. I start frenetically chewing a nicotine tablet.

It helps. I return to my father's narrative.

When I woke up in the morning and looked out of the window, I saw the ship that would take me to Constantinople. It was Turkish, registered with the Machsousé company. Shortly afterward, the red crescent flag was hoisted and I left Sampson with my heart pounding. After thirty-two hours we reached the Bosphorus Strait, the Clashing Rocks of mythology. A wonderful nine-hour voyage through the sound took us to the inlet of Keráteion.

Our ship was immediately surrounded by the rowboats that would take us ashore, next to the Galata

Bridge which joins the old Byzantine city with the new one, known as Péran or Beyoğlu in Turkish.

I gathered my few possessions and hailed a Turkish carriage to get to the home of my aunt Paraskeví, whom I met for the first time. She was a very good person, and treated me like her own child. She had a son called Giángo (Giannis) and a daughter, Athiná.

They lived on Ouzountsarsí in Constantinople. Paraskeví's husband was called Dimitris, but he was better known as the Captain. He had been a cotton wholesaler in the old Byzantine market, which today is called BirTsarsí.

This bazaar had many domes and was completely enclosed, with only four entrances. The dealers traded in cotton, beds, wool, and spices. The stores didn't have doors to close; the goods were left out all night, watched over by special guards.

I was very lucky to get out of Oinoe. Only a few days later the Turkish authorities banned all Christians in coastal towns from traveling overseas. And later, when the Germans invaded, all boys and men from the age of thirteen upward were gathered and taken to the interior of the country, accompanied by gendarmes. They walked for a whole month before they reached the place of their exile. Many died along the way. The survivors were split into labor gangs and built roads to the Russian border.

This was the fate that awaited my former colleagues. I heard that the principal was arrested on suspicion of espionage and was hanged in the square in Oinoe. The poor man died a hard death, and left behind his wife and eight-year-old son.

I thanked my lucky stars that I was so far away from the miseries of war.

In Constantinople I was informed that my father had died of pneumonia. How I grieved because I was unable to be with him in his final hours. He was fifty-seven years old.

My mother had to wait alone for her sons and sons-in-law, who had been exiled and were working in labor camps on the Russian border.

I had no difficulty finding employment in Constantinople. The patriarch, who was responsible for the schools in the Greek community, took me on as a teacher in one of the schools in the city. I stayed there for six years. On health grounds I was not conscripted into the army. In June 1918, the war was approaching its end. After many defeats, the Turkish army had suffered great losses. A general mobilization was announced in order to fill the gaps, which meant that I too had to don a soldier's uniform. I trained for one month in the military academy in Constantinople to become an officer, because I could write and speak Turkish well.

In July 1918 I was sent to the front in Syria as a second lieutenant. I took part in many bloody battles between Haifa and the Jordan River.

I was promoted to lieutenant and awarded the Iron Cross by the German military and the War Medal by the Turkish state.

Not a word more. If it had been me, I would have gone into detail about this precious memory, probably enhancing the story as time went by. Not my father.

In July 1918 I was sent to the front in Syria as a second lieutenant. I took part in many bloody battles between Haifa and the Jordan River.

I was promoted to lieutenant and awarded the Iron Cross by the German military and the War Medal by the Turkish state.

That was all.

How had this happened? What had he done? He spoke so little about the past. He wasn't the kind of man who told stories at the dinner table. There was a kind of defiance in this silence, which I noticed as I grew older. I would look at him, sitting there with his newspaper, and I would think: *There's Dad with his secrets.* It was a thought that both intrigued and frightened me. However, at some point he must have said something, because I had a vague memory of a rescue operation that he had led. I didn't know any more than that. Had many people died? Who had he and his men rescued?

He didn't write a single word about any of that.

I try to imagine the heat in the Jordanian valley, the soldiers' fear, the young lieutenant's determination as he drove them forward, the euphoria when they succeeded, the ceremony in which the Greek second lieutenant with the battle-scarred Turkish army became a lieutenant, complete with a mustache. I don't get very far. I can't see my father in that situation. All I see are images from war movies, although most of those are set in the Second World War.

When the concrete disappears, the banal takes over. That is one of the reasons why we must bear witness. Every memory that is lost is replaced by a cliché. The world of the clichés is a world with amnesia.

It was fortunate that my father had had a photograph taken of himself with the German Iron Cross and the Turkish War Medal pinned to his chest. It was fortunate in many ways: partly because it meant no one could doubt what he had written, and partly because that photograph saved his life after many years. More of that later.

"Not far to go now," my neighbor says. She has noticed that I am no longer reading.

I look out of the window. We are flying over a city; it looks like Thessaloniki. From there to Athens is hardly any distance at all.

I think I ought to be a little more sociable.

"I remember the dear master Sven Lindqvist's exhortation: 'Dig where you stand.' That must be a dangerous piece of advice to give a Greek," I say.

She laughs, and suddenly looks like a young girl. She explains to me that there is almost more life beneath the earth than upon it. The big difference is the noise. Life above ground is noisier.

"The worst thing is that we can't deal with everything we find, so we cover some of it up again, to preserve it for future generations."

What a fantastic piece of information. People spend years, decades, digging things up, only to bury them again because they have no choice. We don't have time to take care of the past. We don't have time to take care of the present. So what do we have time for? Or what do we do with the time we have?

"Modern people are more modern than people," my archaeologist neighbor says.

It could have been an interesting conversation, but the plane is beginning to descend, and my ears are so badly affected that I can't hear a word she says. For the rest of the flight I simply nod in agreement.

THE FIRST DAY

MY MOTHER IS STANDING at the door of her apartment when I step out of the elevator into the dark hallway. She holds the door wide open as if to expand her embrace. But she is not alone. Her neighbor Maria is also standing there with her three children. Dark, silent, with burning eyes. Maria has lost weight since the last time I saw her. She is beautiful.

I am a little confused, just as I am confused writing this. Do I have the right to talk about Maria? Shouldn't I ask her? Once, long ago, I was in the Algerian quarter in Paris, and took some photographs without asking for permission. I was almost lynched. I realized too late that we do what we please with others' faces and bodies, we do what we please with their narrative. In the West we regard one another as occupied territory. We walk around, colonizing the fates of others. We appropriate their suffering, we profit from their misery. Maria is an immigrant from Egypt, a courageous young woman who works like a dog to put food on the table for her children. She is in the process of getting a divorce. Shouldn't I let all this remain her business? Why drag her into my story?

But there she is. If you stand in front of the crocodile's jaws, you will be eaten up. At the same time, she has created an unexpected problem. Who should I greet first—Maria and her children, or my mother? The longed-for reunion has suddenly become a protocol issue. I decide to clear up that matter first. I shake hands with Maria, say hi to the children, and only then do I hug my mother, and she hugs me back. Her embrace has always been bigger than mine, by which I mean that she is able to accommodate me while I cannot return the favor, and it isn't a question of physical shape.

Maria and the children go into their apartment. The little girl, who is dressed as a princess, doesn't take her eyes off me, and edges in backward. Who knows what she sees. Who knows what Maria has told them about me.

"Hi Mom."

"Welcome, my treasure."

I am embarrassed to write this, but that's what she actually says. More of that later.

She reaches down to pick up my suitcase. I stop her.

"I can manage, my son, I can," she assures me.

I wonder when the tears will come.

It is time now. Once we are inside her apartment, she is finally able to show her joy. It is always tearful, as I said earlier.

I know exactly what to do.

"What smells so good?" I ask.

My mother's face immediately lights up, and she dries her eyes. An expression I have never seen on anyone else comes over her. How to describe it?

It is fleeting, it makes a surprising appearance and then it is gone. She narrows her eyes, her eyelids flicker, she purses her lips, wrinkles her nose, her gaze is steady and happy but also a little skeptical, as if to say: You can't fool me, I gave birth to you, I know you inside out, and I might allow myself to be led astray sometimes, but that's not down to you, I do it because I love you so much, so you can enjoy it, but don't get any ideas!

It's hardly surprising that I haven't seen that expression on anyone else. She's the only one who is my mother.

The wonderful smell is coming from what is in the oven, of course.

"As you weren't here at Easter, I saved you some."

It is goat, cut into large chunks and slowly fried, along with potato wedges soaked in melted butter.

"Mom, I don't want that meat with a beard," I say, trying to sound the way I think I sounded when I was three years old.

It is a precious memory that she has of me, but I don't have it myself. The memory is so precious that she feels the need to imitate me, and goes on to tell me that I refused to eat goat when I was little, for that very reason: because it had a beard.

I have heard the story before. It doesn't matter. I am happy to hear it again and again.

The food won't be ready for a little while, so I take

the opportunity to unpack. I have bought her some anti-wrinkle cream and a box of chocolates. At first she says I didn't need to bring her presents, but I know she would be hurt if I showed up with nothing. It's not so much about the gifts themselves, it's more that she doesn't like empty hands.

That's something she often says. "I don't go anywhere with empty hands." It is stronger than her. Going somewhere means going with something in your hands.

To receive and to give. It is the balance between these two actions that constitutes her life, among other things. She even has a theory about it. The more you give, the more you receive. It is an extremely optimistic theory, but she has lived by it for ninety-two years and I have no intention of contradicting her, even though my own theory is significantly more misanthropic. It seems to me that you can give ninety-nine times, but if you don't give on the hundredth occasion, that is what is noted and remembered.

Anyway, my mother goes to the bathroom to try out her new cream, and I watch her go. She has acquired a walking stick since my last visit. She takes small, slightly uncertain steps, and her back is bent. The stick is a jaunty shade of blue. *She's aged*, I think. The question is—how much?

She is moving more quickly when she comes back, her back is straighter and she has a big smile on her face.

"All the wrinkles are gone now," she says.

THE FOOD TASTES DIVINE. The meat is crisp on the outside and tender on the inside, with no trace of the rather acrid smell that goat sometimes has.

"How do you do it?" I ask with my mouth full.

"Your grandfather taught me. I rub the meat with half a lemon. I don't pour lemon juice over it, I rub it in. My father, God rest his soul, knew his stuff. The only thing he couldn't do was look after his money. He drove my mother crazy. 'You have holes in your pockets, old man,' she would complain."

She embarks on a new story about my grandfather's activities. He had inherited a large and attractive piece of land in the middle of the village. Suddenly another family started to build a house there. My grandmother demanded an explanation. Which she got. He had given away the land. "They have children and nowhere to live," he said.

"Oh, who has seen God and not trembled with fear? My mother went crazy, tore at her hair and cursed the day she had married this idiot, while he tried to calm her down. My poor father! His heart was just too big. Otherwise we would be rich today," my mother goes on, then immediately regrets her words. "We are rich. I am rich. Three sons, five grandchildren, four great-grandchildren. And soon I might get more from our girl."

Our girl is my daughter, Johanna, whose unmarried state is a recurring theme.

"She's an adult, Mom. She makes her own decisions," I say, feeling the need to defend my daughter. It really isn't necessary, because my mother is very proud of her and can't believe Johanna's a judge. "Does she really put people behind bars?" she often asks me.

She immediately notices that I don't like this talk of marriage, and puts an end to it.

"The main thing is that she's happy."

The retreat is temporary. The topic will arise several times during the coming days.

It is hardly surprising. For my mother, life is synonymous with having a family, especially for a woman. I have no desire to correct her, to tell her times have changed and so on.

Sometimes it is slightly uncomfortable to live between two different cultures. Family doesn't play the same role in Sweden. Children are raised to be independent—the sooner and the more independent, the better. I remember an incident from my earliest days in Sweden. I was visiting a girl, and her parents invited me to stay for dinner. After the meal, at about seven thirty in the evening, the girl's youngest brother, five years old, stood up and announced that he was going over to a friend's house. There was no outrage, no anxiety, merely a mild exhortation to make sure he didn't stay out too late.

In Greece this would have led to heartrending scenes. A five-year-old, out on his own, in the middle of the night!

This is not a generational issue but a cultural one, based on the weight that Greek and Swedish cultures give to the family. I can understand both positions, I can see good in both, which makes it impossible to embrace one and reject the other. The Greeks become their mothers' sons, while the Swedes become their society's sons.

This is what evokes what I previously referred to as confusion—an existential confusion, which doesn't remain within the four walls of the home. I experience it several times a day. I am simply not Greek enough any longer, nor have I become Swedish enough. I am like Janus: with two faces but only one head.

That head is beginning to feel heavy. I had woken up at three in the morning in order to be at Arlanda Airport by five thirty. My ears still haven't popped, and the two small glasses of wine I have drunk with my meal have taken their toll. My mother has also drunk a thimbleful of wine. I have never seen her drink any more than that.

She notices that I am tired.

"Go and lie down for a while," she says.

"I was going to do the washing up."

There is a long, embarrassed silence, as if I had farted loudly.

I put down my pipe and stand up, ready to clear the table.

She has had enough.

"Sit down," she says impatiently. "This is my job."

Another example of that existential confusion. At home in Sweden I do the washing up, I do the laundry, I clean the house, I iron my shirts and my wife's blouses. The first time I told my mother this, I thought she would praise me. Instead she almost fainted from the shock. She couldn't even speak, she simply shook her head as if she were asking herself what other horrors life held in store for her. When I stay with her, I am not allowed to do any of those tasks.

"Washing up occasionally won't kill me, Mom."

She's not too sure about that.

"As long as I am on my feet, it's my job."

I give in.

"Would you like some fruit? I have strawberries, melon, apples."

"I'm too full!"

"You poor boy! You eat like a bird!"

I don't comment. She has spent her whole life with me trying to fatten me up, but without success.

She starts eating strawberries, covered in sugar. The very sight of them makes me shudder.

"Are they good?"

"Not like they used to be. Your beloved father loved strawberries."

Her eyes are shiny with tears. She can't even mention my father without tears filling her eyes. Did she love him so much, or is it merely the sentimentality of the survivor?

One day I will ask her. But right now I need to sleep.

She has made up the sofa bed for me. The sheets smell wonderful. I lie down with a sense of reverence, as if I am about to be baptized again.

"Everywhere in this world you are a guest, except in your mother's house." That was what my grandmother used to say, and my mother has followed the same mantra. The strange thing is that I agree with them. In this dark room, to which I come once or twice a year, I am at home. Not in my home, but at home. If that hasn't changed in all the years I have lived in Sweden, there is no reason to think that it will ever change. Shortly before I fall asleep, I wonder why I can't hear anything from the kitchen. I know my mother is doing the washing up, but I can't hear a sound.

She is the quietest person in the world. I make a mental note to take up this thread again, and then I fall asleep.

AN HOUR OR SO later I hear my father's voice calling to me. I know that I am not fully awake, and that my father has been dead for twenty-four years. He used to wake me when I was in school, and later when I was on leave from the military. Why do I remember that, such an undramatic thing, when I have forgotten so much else? Sometimes I get the feeling that we don't choose our memories but are chosen by them.

I have a tendency to philosophize a little while I am waking up. Could it be that deep down I haven't come to terms with his death? Occasionally I catch myself wondering when he's going to show up with the newspaper tucked underneath his arm.

He hasn't shown up yet.

While I am waiting, I get up. The apartment is totally silent. I pad along quietly to my mother's room. She is lying in the double bed, sleeping without making a sound. Her mouth is closed, her old hands, marked with liver spots, are resting on the blanket. How does she manage to retain her dignity even in sleep?

I have never seen her naked. I have never been aware of her going to the bathroom or heard her stomach rumble. She can even blow her nose without my hearing her. When my father blew his nose, the entire house shook.

She has never imposed her physicality on us. Is she simply a true Victorian?

No, she isn't even aware that such a thing exists. It's just the way she is, discreet by nature. In spite of her one hundred and eighty pounds she treads lightly upon this earth, her movements are gentle and economical. She doesn't clatter around in the kitchen, she picks things up and puts them down without making any noise. She doesn't crash into the world.

I love the silence that my mother creates around her. It is her hallmark. Unfortunately her children have not inherited this quality. I bump into every door in my way, and my brother speaks as loudly as if we were deaf, which to be fair we are when he has been holding forth for a while.

My maternal grandfather also kept the volume down. This cheerful, chubby man moved as silently as a shadow, and his constant complaint was about the noise everyone around him made.

"Why so much crashbangwallop, my children?" he would say. It was a term he had coined especially for this purpose, and I was so happy to recall it that I began to laugh, with tears in my eyes. As I said, the happiness of the Greek is always tearful.

The last time I saw him alive, he didn't recognize me. I had traveled to the village to say goodbye. I was on my way to Sweden. When I told him who I was, he began to weep in the middle of the village square.

My grandmother reacted with more stoicism.

"Your mother is losing you." That was all she said.

She had considerable experience with loss. Two brothers in America, a daughter in Athens. When my grandfather died, she bent over the coffin and made just one request.

"Come and fetch me, old man, before the year is out."

Before the year was out, my grandmother was fetched. She knew exactly when it was time. On the last day of her life she got up, had a bath, washed her hair, put on her best clothes, then visited her friends and neighbors to say goodbye.

Then she returned home and died.

I GO INTO THE kitchen. The dishes have been washed and neatly stacked to dry. I am longing for a cup of coffee, the kind the Greeks call Greek and the Turks call Turkish. The aroma I grew up with. I can't swear that it's the nicest of smells, but it's the most reassuring. I feel calm as soon as I smell the kind of coffee the Greeks call Greek and the Turks call Turkish.

Making that kind of coffee is an art, even though it looks straightforward. Back in the day, when real cafés still existed, you could order your coffee exactly the way you liked it. There were a number of different options. Here are a few:

"Sweet."

"Very sweet."

"Medium."

"Strong with a little sugar."

"Strong with no sugar."

"Strong with crema in a thin cup."

"Strong with no crema in a thick cup."

"Sweet with air bubbles in a smooth cup."

The way you took your coffee was also significant, because it reflected your character.

Once upon a time I knew exactly which type of people took their coffee sweet and which took it strong, but standing there in my mother's kitchen I have forgotten. One thing I know for certain, though: My mother wants her coffee sweet with lots of bubbles in a smooth cup. I prefer it strong, with a little sugar in a thick cup.

In other words, you can't simply boil up a pot of coffee. I have to make two different kinds, because you can't add the sugar afterward. That destroys the bubbles, which are of great importance—partly for the appearance, and partly for the future.

You might wonder why, of course, but the explanation will come.

When I have finished I peep into my mother's room again. She has heard me, in spite of my efforts to be quiet. She is lying in exactly the same position, but her eyes are open. She smiles when she sees me.

"Did you get some sleep?" she asks.

"I slept like a log."

The answer pleases her.

"In that case it's time for coffee."

"I've already made coffee."

"Oh, my little housekeeper."

"I don't know if it's sweet enough."

That's the risk and it worries her, but she decides to be generous.

"If I have the joy of drinking coffee made by the hands of my child, it doesn't matter what it's like."

Making coffee for her is an exception to the general ban on all household tasks on my part. You might think this is illogical. On the contrary, it is entirely logical. Making coffee for someone is not part of the housework but is covered by the unwritten laws about care and warmth, intimacy and closeness. Small cups of coffee instead of hugs.

It is five o'clock. The sky has cleared and there is heat in the sun. It is the second week in May, the difficult time of year when it starts to get warmer outside than inside.

I carry the tray out onto the balcony, with its iron table and uncomfortable chairs. They have been there for as long as I can remember. My mother has refused to sit on them for as long as I can remember. She has her own chair, with a couple of cushions on the seat.

On the balconies opposite everyone is already busy watering their plants. We have to wait for another hour or so, because we are facing the sun.

My mother comes out with her hair freshly combed. She smells of lemons.

"Excellent coffee," she says.

The neighbor opposite calls out to her.

"Welcome to your son, Antonia."

"Thank you so much, Katerina."

The mothers talk over my head, four floors up, as if I don't exist.

It doesn't matter. I wave to indicate my thanks.

When I light my pipe, my mother says, "You look like your grandfather, although you're half his weight."

Tirelessly she arranges her world, that is to say her family. This one and this one talk like that one and that one, this one looks like that one, this one walks like that one, and so on in a constant state of flux. She strengthens the bonds as best she can. She watches over the past, as I said earlier. She can point to each and every person's place in the chain.

The truth is that I take some comfort from knowing that I resemble my grandfather, although I can't really explain why.

You might get the impression that she doesn't care about anything else. That isn't true. My mother has a passionate interest in politics, and follows every debate she can. She has opinions on most things. On the way children are brought up these days, on the behavior of young women, on divorce, on the heartless men who leave their families to follow "their bird," that is to say their penis. Her political ideology is simple: Even the poor must be allowed to live. Her heart is vaguely to the left of center, but her faith received a blow when the leader of the Social Democrats got divorced in order to marry a woman thirty years his junior. She is not sufficiently sophisticated to distinguish between solidarity as a political program and as a matter of personal morality.

"A human being is cast in a single piece," she sometimes says. "And if he or she is not, then have nothing to do with them."

I don't entirely agree with her, but I don't disagree either, even though this view also affects me. My youthful dream of a moral transparency turned out to be just that: a dream. Compromises, self-deception, and lies, from white to pitch-black, became inescapable from an early stage.

In other words I sit in silence, drink my coffee, smoke my pipe, and think about how many times like this we might have left.

We will soon find out.

We have finished our coffee. My mother picks up her empty cup and moves it around like a wine taster. Then she quickly turns it upside down onto the saucer. A tiny amount of the grounds trickles out.

I do the same thing, but don't manage to turn it over with the same lightning speed. Far too much of the grounds run out onto the saucer.

"Oh no, you poor thing! Now there'll be nothing left to read."

She can see the future in the patterns the coffee grounds make on the inside of the cup. It is known as "reading the cup," and it is a beloved game that we have played for a long time. I have occasionally expressed my doubts about this method, but have been put in my place with a reminder that Aunt Chrisi read in my mother's cup fifty years ago that her youngest son—me—would make her famous throughout the whole country.

So does she really believe?

It's not that simple. There is always the possibility of "misreading," but one thing is for certain, both she and I are noticeably relieved if the cup is good, if it shows successful trips, a healthy income, lasting love, good health.

Strangely enough, my cup usually shows exactly that.

The same is true on this occasion. The short text, that is to say the small amount of coffee grounds left in my cup, forms long, airy, attenuated patterns.

"Oh my oh my! There's money here," my mother says.

I let out a long breath.

"What does yours say?" I ask.

She concentrates on her cup.

"That's remarkable! Look at this, you doubting Thomas!"

She points to a shape that looks like a sperm.

"It's crystal clear—a visit! And my youngest son is visiting me," she says triumphantly.

The farmer looks up at the sky more often than he looks down at the ground. He knows what to expect from the ground, but not from the sky. Human beings have always asked themselves what tomorrow will bring. They have asked the gods, the prophets, the wise men. They have interpreted the song and flight of the birds, the height and direction of smoke, the charred bones of sacrificed animals. They have read cards, crystal balls, constellations, the palms of their own hands.

The day we stop worrying about the future is the day we stop taking care of our memories. It may be that both of these activities are pointless, if it is pointless to be a human being. Perhaps that was what the archaeologist on the plane meant by "modern people," that they only worry about the present, or rather for the moment.

We stay where we are for a long time. My mother tells me what a curious child I was. I picked up everything I found and asked, "What is this and what does it do?"

And she tells me about the day I poured a whole packet of salt into the stew she was making.

And about the competitions my brother organized in the hallway at home between me and the cat, to find out which of us was fastest. He would hold on to the cat's back paws as I adopted the starting position, then he would count to three and let go.

I remember the cat, but nothing else. One thing is for sure: I never won. I have heard these stories before, but that has no significance. You can't dismiss the sea because you have seen it before.

In these moments my mother becomes a great sea that surrounds me without threatening me. I listen to her voice and think about something else, present and absent at the same time.

Have my children experienced this sense of security, the deepest of all?

Or is it a sense of security that is only linked to my Greekness? In other words, I become calm when I am allocated my place in the chain.

I may be sixty-eight years old, but I am and will remain my mother's youngest son.

LATER THAT EVENING I take a stroll around the area. My area, Gyzi the red. It lies to the left of Alexandras Avenue, which was regarded as the outskirts of the city when I was a child. There are several hills and a riverbed that divided it in two. Over time it has gotten closer to the city, or the city has gotten closer. It was a workers' district. The left has always been in the majority. During the German occupation, many people from here were killed. During the civil war that followed, even more died. Others ended up in camps and jails. The first two football players I fell in love with were well-known for their left-wing politics. The playing field for my team, Panathinaikos with the green strip, was opposite the jails, where political prisoners hung out at the windows every Sunday when there was a game, shouting to us as we walked by to find out the result.

It was to this area that I came in 1946, when I was forced to leave my village, Molai, at eight years old. The buildings were peppered with bullet holes, there were more women dressed in black than anyone else, orphaned children wandered around, making a paltry living by cleaning shoes or running errands. They lived on their own in a deserted house. Refugees from Asia Minor lived in wooden or metal barracks a short distance away from the dried-up riverbed. On hot summer nights they slept outdoors, and my friends and I would sneak around in the hope of seeing some naked flesh.

I lived here from the age of eight until I left my country when I was twenty-five. My whole life before I emigrated took place around here. My first kiss, my first poem, my first rebellion, my first true friends.

I still don't feel the need to talk about them, not even to myself. The memories come and go, but I make no attempt to hold on to them. This area is my river of oblivion. I sail on it with my light shoes, stealing glances at those who wave to me from its banks. There's Mary. Green eyes, black hair, wild, with a six-cylinder brain. I sail on. There's Maria. Blue eyes, blond hair, even wilder, and with a slightly twisted brain, like a free kick by Beckham. There's Kostas. Black eyes, black hair, burning in more ways than one. I sail on. At the next bend Diagoras and Giannis are waiting, always together. Tall, beautiful boys, more talented than they realized. I sail on.

I want to remember without remembering. I want to be my memories.

THE AREA HAS CHANGED. If I take the topographical features first, which are also the most tangible, I can see that the surrounding hills have practically been eaten up by construction. The broad ravine that carried away all the rainwater has been covered in asphalt. Buildings have been demolished and replaced with tower blocks. For example, my first home in Athens is gone. The simple taverna where we could always eat our fill for next to nothing is gone.

Then we have the demographic changes. In the play area most of the children and the adults with them are speaking Albanian. There are three Albanian families in my mother's apartment block, and as I said earlier, her neighbor Maria is from Egypt. In the square I see many tall, blond girls coming and going. They are probably from Albania.

It has happened fast. From almost zero immigration there are now more than a million immigrants in Greece. Most are in the big cities, and most are Albanians.

The process has not been painless, but it has worked. Most of them have learned Greek, and the children attend Greek schools.

"The little girl down in the basement is top of her class," my mother told me.

Maybe we could learn something about the dynamics of immigration.

"The Albanians are the future of Greece," says the waiter who brings my ouzo at one of the many cafés in the square, my own Gyzi square, bigger than my heart but not too big to fit inside it. The starting block of my dreams.

I glance covertly at the young Albanian men and women sitting in the café. I left here fully laden for another country. They have come here fully laden from their own country.

It is a shame that we cannot tell one another's stories.

We mustn't close our eyes to the problems. But I don't want to talk about the imbecile of a principal who prevented an Albanian girl, the best student in the school, from carrying the flag at the ceremony to mark the end of the academic year.

I would rather talk about the girl, who proved herself worthy of such an honor.

Although I don't know too much about her.

Because in Greece the same thing applies as in Sweden. Officially, immigration is a problem. Unofficially, it's a solution.

I hardly manage to formulate the thought when I realize for the first time in my life how prophetic poetry can be. It is a kind of revelation, like being saved.

Konstantinos Kavafis—Constantine P. Cavafy—was something of a recluse in Alexandria in the nineteenth and twentieth centuries. In one of his poems he describes a town waiting for the barbarians. The inhabitants preparing to receive them, the politicians polishing ceremonial speeches, the tension rising with each verse. But the barbarians do not come. Which is a pity because, Kavafis says, "Those people were a kind of solution."

That is our situation.

Europe stands motionless, waiting for the barbarians. We no longer ask ourselves who the barbarians are.

Is it possible that we ourselves are the barbarians?

WHEN I RETURN TO my mother's apartment I find that my brother, his wife, and their son have arrived. After the ritual welcome kisses and the obligatory questions about one another's health, we move on to politics, football, the national economy, and many other things.

My sister-in-law, my nephew, and I drink whiskey. My brother and my mother don't touch strong drink; they have another cup of coffee.

My sister-in-law has a specialty. She slices carrots and pours lemon juice over them. She insists this is the best accompaniment to a good whiskey.

Believe it or not, she is right. And you never get a hangover.

My mother doesn't say much, but suddenly she sighs loudly. "Just imagine if the others were here!"

There is a brief silence as if we are all trying to work out what this would mean. I come to the conclusion that around twenty people are missing. This is my mother's first lineup. Some are alive and doing well elsewhere— for example, my wife, my children and grandchildren. Some are dead: her husband, her stepson, her brother, her parents.

Some have been dead for a very long time. But not to her. The only problem is that they're not here. Although there is nothing to stop us from imagining that they are here. Life would be perfect. If only everyone were here.

My mother and my sister-in-law quickly put together a light supper. Tomato salad, feta, olives, little fried sausages, an omelet. My brother, his son, and I drink beer. My sister-in-law opts for a glass of wine, and asks my mother if she would like one too.

"No thank you. I've already drunk a lot today."

She is referring to the thimbleful she had with lunch, but suddenly she misses my son, whose name is Markus—the same as the wine.

"Actually, I will have a drop for my Markus, who isn't here."

My son lived with her for a whole summer when he decided he wanted to study Greek in Athens. She has lots of stories about him, but one is a particular favorite. She and Markus had gone to the seaside. After a swim it was time to eat something at the taverna near the shore. Markus changed into long pants before sitting down at the table. My mother's girlfriends couldn't believe their eyes. Such a well-brought-up boy! They had imagined that Swedes were completely wild.

"I smiled to myself and thought: You poor souls, in which cradle were you rocked? Their husbands were sitting there with their bellies out, pubic hair on show—it was enough to make anyone lose their appetite!—while my Swedish grandson was a real gentleman."

And that's how it continues. She misses her husband, my wife, my daughter, her lost stepson, his children, and so on. Every name has a story attached, and every mouthful of food has a name attached.

Mom, how do you manage to carry so much love without falling apart? I think.

But perhaps I am wrong. Perhaps it is this love that holds her together. She names the bread she is eating after those she loves in a kind of heathen communion, and I don't believe that God, if he exists, would mind at all.

MY BROTHER AND HIS family leave at about ten thirty, and my mother and I are alone once more. It is a little chilly, but we stay on the balcony for a while longer. The steel-blue light of various televisions streams toward us from the apartments opposite.

"How was your walk? Did you go past our old home?"

"No. I might go that way tomorrow."

She sighs deeply. "We've been through so much."

"It's over now, Mom."

She considers this. "My poor son! When I see children today, the toys they have, their clothes, the money their parents spend on extra lessons and foreign languages, and you could hardly fit your legs under the table where you sat studying. 'Mom, there isn't enough room,' you used to say. But still you sat there as if you were screwed to the chair."

I remember that too. It was my final year of high school, and I had finally grown taller. I did my homework at a small, low table. I've never forgotten that table.

"Do you still have it?"

"It's next to your bed."

"That little one?" I actually didn't remember that it was *so* small.

I have to check. I remove the telephone sitting on top of it, take off the cloth that my mother no doubt embroidered herself, the smooth surface reflects the light just as it did fifty years ago. I pick up a book I have with me, place it on the table, sit down on a chair and try to fit my legs under the table. Impossible.

"We have both grown older," I say to the table with a smile, while at the same time I feel my Greek bitterness rising within me like a spring tide. That's what I call it, because I don't know what else to call it. I can't describe it either. However, I get the impression that the first word most Greeks learn to say is not "Mommy" or something similar, but "why." This unanswered "why" marks my life in Greece like a series of land mines.

Suddenly I am in a hurry to get back to my mother.

"Shall we go in and watch the news?" she says.

Why are old people so interested in the news? My father-in-law is the same age as my mother, and he also has a passionate interest in the news. We sometimes have dinner together, but at about twenty past seven he becomes restless, looks at his watch, and says, "Time's getting on." He is thinking about *Rapport*, the evening news program.

My father was the same, although in his case it was the radio, of course. The first thing he did in the morning and the last thing he did at night was to listen to the news.

I can't help putting the question to my mother. "Why do you care so much about the news?"

"I want to check it out," she says in an attempt to sound younger.

"Check what out?"

"How the world is getting along without me."

Maybe when you're ninety-two years old you take on the responsibility of being everyone's mother.

We watch the news and my mother is intensely involved in what is going on around the world. She comments, snorts, shakes her head. There are accidents, bombs in Baghdad, bombs in Israel, floods.

"A bad year," she says. "God has grown tired of us."

It is time to go to bed.

I get ready first. I say "Good night," lie down on the narrow sofa bed.

My mother gets ready after me. I don't hear a sound. Then suddenly she gives a huge, demonstrative yawn. "Tonight I will sleep peacefully."

I know what she means. She is actually a little bit scared of sleeping alone. I understand perfectly. I had felt the same fear during my first few years in Stockholm. What if I died in my sleep, who would find me?

"Me too," I call back to her.

I had intended to read some more of my father's words.

But I am too tired. It isn't so much that I am sleepy, it is just that I can't take in any more. It has been a long day. For some strange reason it's always like this when I return to Athens. Long days. I wonder why? Is it because my youth is lying in wait? Am I afraid of meeting ghosts and nightmares from those days? Or am I afraid that nothing will be awakened within me? That the past is gone forever, and my heart is as empty as a walnut shell with no kernel inside?

I really don't know.

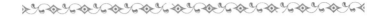

THE SECOND DAY

AT FIVE O'CLOCK IN the morning I am woken by the doves cooing in the courtyard. I feel rested, and want a cup of coffee. On the way to the kitchen I hear my mother's voice: "Are you up?"

How can she have heard me? I have been as quiet as a mouse. But that's how she is. I know that after all the years as her son. However late I came home, however careful I tried to be, she always woke up.

"Yes—I'm going to make a cup of coffee. Would you like one?"

"What's the point of getting up at this hour? Are we going to feed the hens?"

I go into her room. Her night-light is shining on an icon of the Virgin Mary, and my parents' wedding wreath. I sit down on the bed.

"Sit down my child, my little night bird."

"Night bird" is one of the names she has given me over the years, precisely because I get up early.

She takes my hand in hers. We sit in silence for a long time, then she says, "I know you're longing for your pipe. Off you go! I'm going back to sleep for a while, now I have my little boy with me."

"I'm going back to bed too," I say.

But I don't. Instead I take out my father's text again and carry on translating. I had left him as a newly promoted lieutenant, decorated with the German Iron Cross and the Turkish War Medal, somewhere in the Jordanian valley.

Unfortunately I suffered from a bleeding stomach ulcer and spent fifteen days in a field hospital. After that I was given a month's leave in Constantinople. I returned to my school. Meanwhile the Turks retreated toward Damascus. Forty thousand men were captured by the British, and the British general Allenby occupied the Syrian capital on October 1, 1918. The Turkish army laid down its arms. On October 30 the peace treaty between the victorious Allies and the defeated Turks was signed. In accordance with the terms of this treaty, units from the British, French, Italian, and Greek armies were posted in Constantinople.

In January 1920 I married Maria Tortopides. I was thirty years old, and my bride was twenty. Her father came from a village by the Black Sea but had emigrated to Constantinople where he learned to make blankets. During the First World War he bought secondhand wool and cotton from poor families, who sold everything in order to avoid starving to

death. Then he sold it to a German Austrian company
that made military uniforms. In that way my father-
in-law amassed a considerable fortune. He owned
a three-story house in the district of Kontoskali in
Constantinople. I moved in there after the wedding.

My mother-in-law was called Elisavet, and came
from Platana by the Black Sea. My parents-in-law had
four children, two boys and two girls. They were nice
people, and living with them was very pleasant.

There were two schools in Kontoskali, one for boys
and one for girls. I was transferred to the boys' school
straight after the wedding. There were nine teachers.
The principal was a mature pedagogue with a great
deal of experience, noble, obliging, always smiling, with
an extremely well-kept beard, Mr. Tourgoutis.

It strikes me that my father was describing this teacher
as he himself would have wanted to be described in the
future, minus the beard.

The future! Always the future! That was my father's
tense in life—either the future, or at least the historic present. A strange little man. He remembered everything, and
yet he always moved on. For most of the rest of us, not least
for me, forgetting is the price of moving on. Not him. He
carried his baggage on his back, so to speak, but he only
opened it when I asked him to.

Why did he do that?

I am horrified to realize the truth. There was no more
future. He was over eighty years old, worn out, weary, and
he was writing his will; he didn't have much else to leave

behind. But he would leave a will so that it could be used in the future. My father wanted me to use this material.

"What a cunning person you were, Dad," I say quietly.

He has been dead for a long time, yet I am still doing what he wanted.

I always had. I did well in every school I attended, because I knew that was what he wanted without him needing to say it. I had resisted the temptations of the emigrant so that he wouldn't be ashamed of me. I had adopted his political ideology, his thirst for knowledge, his spartan lifestyle. One thing I hadn't made mine: his love for the future. In that respect I was my mother's son. My time is the past.

Although sometimes the present makes itself known. Suddenly my mother is standing in front of me. I hadn't heard her coming.

"Do you never get tired of reading?"

This is a ritual question. I have been subjected to it all my life, and not just as a question but also an assertion when she was speaking to others: "This child of mine never gets tired of reading." For her, reading is not a suspect pastime, as it is for many others, but rather incomprehensible. What is it that exists in books? Everything important is to be found outside books. Loving your family, living with sorrow over what you have lost, forgiving past injustices. But that's not the main issue. The main issue is that reading cuts off the reader from his surroundings. That's what she can't really handle—being put to one side, dumped for the sake of a book. So she must immediately start the campaign to retake lost ground.

"What do you want to eat? What has your soul been longing for?" she asks.

I don't even have time to answer.

"Why am I asking you? I know. I will make lalagides, or would you prefer loukoumades?"

Both are magical words. They refer to a kind of waffle, fried in oil then dipped in honey. The difference between them is the shape. Lalagides are flat, loukoumades are round, but they both encapsulate the Sunday mornings of my childhood. I can't eat either without becoming ten years old again.

I have no desire to start the day by becoming a child again.

At the same time, I have no desire to start the day by preventing my mother from being a mother. Luckily, I know her weak points.

"Mom, I would love to eat both, but I think we should wait until my brother is here. It will be more fun then."

She is silent in the face of this incontrovertible truth, even though she is not convinced by its authenticity. I know her weaknesses, but she knows my little lies. She looks at me with suspicion but gives in. We make do with feta and bread.

My mother has slept well and is unusually talkative. She entertains me with stories about her grandmother.

"Can you believe it—I've forgotten her name," I say.

"Paraskeví. Paraskeví Kofinou. She came from a big family."

I ask her to tell me more. I never tire of finding out more about these people, so far away in the past, and yet so astonishingly close. They are links in the same chain.

My great-grandmother's husband was well off, but lost everything because he stepped in as guarantor for some people from the village who emigrated to America and couldn't afford to pay for their tickets. They never repaid him, and he had to take the consequences. It cost him his life. At first he thought everything would work out. He tried to borrow money from others, but no one was prepared to help him. He became increasingly depressed, and in the end he fell ill and died.

My great-grandmother was a young widow with four children to take care of. However, she had "the gift"—an equally powerful and inexplicable ability to cure people of all kinds of ailments, from headaches to infertility.

No herb or plant held any secrets for her, and she was also an excellent midwife. No one, mother or child, had died in her care. People came to her from far and wide—including suitors, whom she chased away with a shotgun. Fortunately, instead of pellets she used coarse salt.

There was one who was particularly persistent, and one summer night he climbed over her wall. My great-grandmother was not afraid and didn't call for help. Instead she fetched her shotgun and aimed at his backside as he was about to clamber down into the yard. She didn't miss, and from then on the man was known as "the black bottom."

"Are you sure he was called 'the black bottom'?" I ask my mother eagerly.

"As sure as we're sitting here."

There is a reason for my eagerness. A while ago I had reached the conclusion that a human life follows a narrative set from the beginning. It happens as it happens in this world, because it cannot happen in any other way. At least not within the framework of a certain culture, and each distinct culture is simply a narrative about the world. What befell the unknown suitor also befell the great hero Heracles. He too was known as "the black bottom." This was a beautiful example of the power and consistency of Greek myth. Vain men do not lose their lives but are subjected to ridicule, and they have been subjected to it for more than three thousand years. If the suitor and my great-grandmother had been born within a different tradition, she would have aimed at a different part of his body, for example his testicles.

She never remarried. Her two sons went to America and never returned.

"What were they called?" I wonder.

"The elder one was Demosthenes. He earned quite a bit of money, and always sent a few dollars to his mother and sisters every month. He was the one who sent the blue bathrobe I gave you when you went to Sweden."

"I still have it. I always take it with me when I travel."

"The clothes they made back then! It must be over sixty years old."

"And the other brother?"

"Konstantis. He became a wrestler. He never sent any money, just newspaper articles about himself. For a while he was famous all over America, but then he disappeared. No one knows what became of him. He was a fine chap, I've seen pictures, vanity running down the legs of his pants. Demosthenes, on the other hand, wanted to get back to the old days, but he had a woman who didn't want to hear a word about Greece. Aunt Chrisi saw it in my coffee cup. 'You have a close relative who is on his way here, but someone is stopping him,' she said, clear as a bell. My poor mother waited in vain for her brother. I felt so sorry for her."

"She had her sister."

"She died young, she wasn't much more than a child."

"Do you remember her name?"

"No. My grandmother hardly ever spoke of her."

The conversation has suddenly become tragic, and my mother doesn't want to feel sad on a morning like this, when she has her youngest son at home. This makes her ask, "Where has your brother gotten to? Didn't he say he was going to drop by?"

"I'm not sure, but I was going to call him."

I have hardly finished the sentence when the phone rings.

"That'll be him," my mother says.

She is right. It is my brother; he doesn't want anything special, just to see how we are.

We are fine.

"Ask Mom if she needs anything from the store."

"Mom," I shout. "Stelios wants to know if you need anything from the store."

"No, I have everything. Is he coming over?"

"Are you coming over?" I ask my brother.

"Not if she doesn't need anything. I'll drop by this afternoon."

"He'll drop by this afternoon," I inform my mother.

"Good. Then I'll make loukoumades."

Although before it is time for loukoumades, she has to make a start on lunch. I leave her in the kitchen and go and sit on the balcony to jot down our conversation.

Five minutes later she appears with another cup of coffee for me.

"That wasn't necessary," I say unkindly.

She doesn't dignify such nonsense with an answer, but simply strokes my hair.

"You've never learned to comb your hair properly."

Then she returns to the kitchen, walking carefully but not shuffling.

Stick to the truth! It's enough that you're spying on her, you don't need to make stuff up, I tell myself as I start writing.

I HAVE ALWAYS BEEN able to write under virtually any circumstances, and absolutely anywhere, even if my situation has become much more comfortable over the years. There is, however, one place where I can't sit without writing: my mother's balcony. It is as if there is a story waiting for me, and there always has been.

In other words, it isn't many minutes before I finish my brief notes and give myself up to something completely different.

Suddenly in my head I hear a sentence I've never heard before. I feel like writing it down, but I don't do it.

I realize immediately that this sentence could be the start of my next book. My happiness is so great that I have to bite my lips to avoid yelling out loud. But I don't write it down. I don't want to set it in stone just yet. I don't know if it's a butterfly or a larva. I will have to wait. Give it time.

Where has this sentence come from? Where has it been hiding until now?

I have my suspicions. For a long time my main preoccupation has been Greek mythology. Gods and goddesses, demigods and demigoddesses, heroes and heroines, dreadful monsters, cruel fates, and more of the same have invaded my head. I was living in a world that was unfinished, that was being created laboriously in a bitter battle between chance and necessity.

In such a world the day could easily begin in the west and the night in the east, if the sun god woke with a hangover and set off in the wrong direction. Nothing unusual, in other words.

And yet this thought has been removed from our minds after several thousand years of indoctrination in more rational explanations, which fortunately haven't reached my mother's balcony. There it has survived.

That is probably why I can't be there without writing. I am simply ambushed by all the real and unreal worlds that gather there. She is the one who waters this strange garden with her unique mixture of the tangible and the intangible, her belief in prophets she likes and her skepticism when it comes to those she doesn't like. She believes in God more than the Devil, although it is because of the latter that she wishes she had eyes in the back of her head. Spending time in the same room as my mother is like spending time in many worlds simultaneously. She makes me become the eyes in the back of her head that she wishes she had.

That is one conclusion.

The other is that I can't stick to the truth for very long.

IT IS PROBABLY TIME to rejoin my mother. She is sitting in the kitchen with a pile of grotesquely huge globe artichokes in front of her. She appears to be at something of a loss.

"Look at these! How am I going to prepare them? Doesn't your brother know about my hands yet?"

My brother knows about her hands, but what could he do? He had bought what was available.

But my mother is right too. She has small hands, and these monster artichokes needed something much bigger. As if that wasn't bad enough, she uses a blunt, ancient knife—the one she has always used.

"Why don't you use the knife Gunilla gave you?" I ask. My wife gave her a really sharp Swedish knife.

"I'm peeling artichokes, not slaughtering an ox," is her unreasonable response. The truth is that the sharp knife frightens her. It is still in its case, unused. Sometimes she shows it to friends and acquaintances, boasting about her daughter-in-law's kindness—but it is never used.

"I prefer my little knife," she says.

She battles on stubbornly, assuring me that if the artichokes aren't ready in time for lunch, she has a chicken she can cook instead.

I can't hide the fact that I sometimes find her fretting about food a little wearisome.

"Don't worry, Mom. We're not living under the occupation anymore."

I am of course referring to the German occupation during the Second World War, when we actually starved.

"A person who has gone hungry in the past is always afraid of hunger," she replies. "Your late father was afraid of hunger until the day he died. His only consolation was that you were over in Sweden. 'If starvation comes again, wife, we will go to our son in Sweden,' he used to say."

I also remember the hunger, although I was little and always got something to eat. Often almonds.

So instead of arguing with her, I help out with the artichokes. When we have finished, she says, "Now wash your hands. There's acid in artichokes."

"What about you?"

"My hands are used to them."

The dish she is preparing is called "artichokes à la polita." I don't know what that means, neither does she, but she knows how to make it. Above all she knows how to mix eggs and lemon to create a harmonious flavor, where neither egg nor lemon is dominant, but the perfect combination of both.

Everything is in the pan now, bubbling away a little too fiercely, in my opinion.

"Is it supposed to be boiling like this?"

"Yes. Vegetables need to be boiled fast and for a short time with salt in the water, meat should be simmered gently for a long time with salt added at the end. Fish shouldn't be boiled at all, just dropped into very hot salted water for a few minutes."

"Wait a minute. I need to write all that down."

I fetch my notebook. My mother eyes me with suspicion.

"You're working on a new book, aren't you?"

"No," I lie. "I'm just gathering material."

"Because if you're writing about me, I don't want sex and swearing on every single page."

"Calm down, Mom."

"Just so you know. You can't fool me, my little squirrel!"

I knew I wouldn't be able to fool her.

"Okay, so now I know. Maybe I'll write a cookbook. Can you go through those instructions again please?"

She claps her hands, delighted.

"The most important thing is to love those you're cooking for," she says. "And don't forget to dance in front of the pan!"

"Are you kidding me?"

"Not at all. Unhappy cooks are the most common cause of bad food. And another thing, before I forget. When your brother arrives, I want you to praise him for the fantastic artichokes he bought for us. That will make him happy."

"But you complained about them."

"Complaining about artichokes is one thing—complaining about my son is an entirely different matter."

"I understand. Would you like a cup of coffee?"

"Made by your hands, yes indeed," she says, taking my hand between hers.

She goes out onto the balcony. The pan is in its place, a mild aroma rising from it. I put the coffee on, and to be on the safe side I execute a few dance steps in front of the stove.

WHY DID SHE CALL me "squirrel"? Why not some other creature? My little bunny rabbit or my little donkey, if it has to be an animal.

I have already hinted at the explanation, when I wrote about my great-grandmother aiming her shotgun at her would-be suitors.

My mother lives her life in the Greek narrative about life. The squirrel has not always been a squirrel. Once upon a time, long long ago, it was a young, fair-haired woman with blue eyes. How do we know this? We have her name. She was called Galinthias, which actually means fair-haired.

Galinthias was best friends with a woman who was in labor and was suffering terribly because the goddesses were preventing her from giving birth. Galinthias stepped in and tricked the goddesses, enabling the baby to be born. As a punishment she was turned into a squirrel.

My mother does not know this. It doesn't matter. The story has conquered her by surviving in everyday language, by gradually becoming a part of everything we inherit, even though we are not aware of it.

This is exactly what we forget so easily when we are discussing art or literature. We tend to regard such things as decorative activities, when in fact they are at the heart of the life we live.

If you are an author you can easily become paralyzed by this realization, but you can also experience the greatest joy that is ever granted to a human being: the joy of tricking the gods as Galinthias did, and allowing another world to be born.

If you think about this too much, you can end up with big problems. I end up with a minor problem: the coffee boils over.

I rescue the situation as best I can and carry the coffee out onto the balcony. Dark clouds are approaching from the west.

"It's going to be cold," my mother says.

"How come?"

"I can feel it on my nose."

"On your nose?"

"Yes. If my nose feels cold, then it's going to be cold. Feel it, you'll see."

I feel her nose. She has a small upturned nose, with very thin nostrils. When I was a teenager and my nose was growing faster than any other part of my body, I dreamed of having a nose like my mother's. I had inherited my father's nose. Fleshy and bulbous, it almost looked obscene.

"You're right, it's cold," I say.

"Dogs always have cold noses," my mother informs me.

The clouds are quickly getting darker.

"It's going to rain."

"Maybe I've got time to stretch my legs before it starts."

"Good idea. Stretch them while you've still got them."

My mother has problems with her legs. She no longer goes out unless my brother is with her. It's not just that she gets tired quickly and has pain in her back and legs—she is also afraid of falling. The sidewalks and streets in the city can be uneven and are not to be trusted. I have experienced this myself, and will experience it again.

And yet she misses the local area. She misses going to the grocery store to do some shopping and chat for a while with Emilia, who has four unmarried daughters at home and a husband who works from four o'clock in the morning until ten o'clock at night, every day of the week, all year round.

"But he's bought apartments for all his girls. And they're pretty girls. What on earth are they waiting for?"

She misses the baker who flirts with her and pays her compliments, assuring her that no one could possibly believe she's over ninety. "Not a day over seventy," he always says.

"Do you know how much these people like me?" my mother asks. "And I love them too."

She tells me that the stylist who has cut her hair for more than forty years, and is now a comfortably-off pensioner, comes to the salon just for her sake. He is old too, but "he still has an eagle eye, and an almost personal relationship with every single hair on my head."

Everyone knows her. She has lived in the area for longer than anyone else. The Albanian four-year-old in the basement beams with joy when she sees her. "Grandma, Grandma!" the child calls out as she runs into my mother's arms.

"I love that little girl. Do you remember when we lived in a basement?"

How could I forget? That was our family's most difficult time, at the beginning of the 1950s. The civil war had just ended with victory for the Right. The jails were full of political prisoners. So were the concentration camps. My half brother was in one of them. My mother cried often. My father worked double shifts. My older brother was constantly either unhappily or happily in love, and in both cases he stayed out late at night. My mother always left a salad for him to eat when he got home—tomatoes, cucumber, and feta cheese. The first time he had sex with a girl, he woke me up in the middle of the night and pointed to his cock inside his underpants. "If only you knew what he's been up to!" he said. I didn't know, so I had started writing poems instead. I started writing poems before I started masturbating. That says it all.

No, I'm wrong. That doesn't say it all. In fact it says nothing. But I can't, I am not yet ready to talk about those years, about the bitterness we heard in our mothers' voices without understanding it.

What should I say about Litsa, who called to her only son each afternoon in a monotone, castrated of every emotion? It still breaks my heart today.

What should I say about the police constables who boxed our ears when they had nothing else to do?

What should I say about the Sunday school where the revered priest terrorized us with the only sin we could not avoid? We weren't even allowed to enjoy our solo "handiwork."

Our basement was much better than the one in which the Albanian family were living, with windows looking out onto a courtyard where a young fig tree grew, laden with glorious figs. However, our landlord was very strict, and we didn't dare touch them.

"He's gone now," my mother says. "He wasn't a bad person, he just had an exaggerated sense of ownership, as your late father used to say."

The Albanian family's basement is a dump, with its only window at street level.

"Those poor souls never dare to open it," my mother tells me. "They do everything in that one room. They cook, they eat, they sleep. And yet. If you see them out and about on Sunday afternoons with their child, you will say, 'What fine folk are these.' Well-dressed, clean and tidy, proud of one another. As far as the girl is concerned, there is only one thing to say: She is a princess. Our fat heifers moan all day that there isn't enough money, and they daren't have children because they want a career. A career as what, may I ask? Test mattresses? Oh, if only I had a whip!"

We are a family with strong dictatorial tendencies. My brother dreams of inventing the automatic slap across the face. As soon as someone thinks, says, or does something dumb, a slap would be delivered to the person in question. I share his dream. Meanwhile, our mother longs for a whip with which to create order. Her grandmother was the same, as was her brother.

The only true democrats were my father, who believed in enlightenment, and my grandfather, who didn't believe in anything.

It may be that my mother has become the area's memory, in a way. "Growing older means having too little to do and too much to remember," she says sometimes, with no hint of complaint. Although she misses those who are gone, for example Master Antonis, who was always around. He was a true friend of the householder, specializing in the things we often forget to buy. Even forgetfulness has its systematic side.

She misses her female friends. They are all gone. She often talks about them, tells stories about them and their husbands, who are also gone. She keeps an eye on how things are going for their children and grandchildren.

"Do you remember that time when Amalia went for a pee, and a turkey bit her on the bottom?" she says, laughing.

"No," I reply. I am also laughing. I remember Amalia, but not the turkey.

"She was an imposing woman. She walked with her back as straight as if she had swallowed a poker. When she went shopping, a lot of people took the opportunity to pinch her bottom in the crush. So she was used to it. She went straight to Mrs. Vassiliki, who owned the turkey, and said, 'Your husband pinching my bottom is one thing, but you need to keep the turkey under control.'"

She doesn't tell the story quite so coherently on this occasion. She starts laughing in advance, and by the time she gets to the end she can barely speak. I am laughing too, but mainly because she is laughing. Women who laugh like that are a blessing. You don't usually get to hear the punch line, but you laugh anyway.

My mother has taken another step back. Now she is thinking about our first home in Athens, when we stayed with Aunt Chrisi and her family. It was 1946, the civil war was raging, my father was out of work, my half brother was doing his military service, my older brother was in high school, the same school I attended a few years later. I was eight years old, skinny, bowlegged due to vitamin deficiency, and scared, because the boys and girls in the big city were so much more experienced than me, who had just arrived from my village. We all had problems fitting in with our new environment, except my mother. She quickly made friends, and those women remained her friends all their lives. She was thirty-two years old at the time, as pretty as a picture, and I guarded her jealously.

But the greatest miracle was Aunt Chrisi, who simply opened her home to us. She was the sister of my father's first wife, and the gentlest person life has ever brought me. We were supposed to stay for a few days, but we were there for several years.

"The house isn't there anymore," my mother says.

"I know. There's hardly anything of our district left."

"Do you remember when Meri crashed into the milk cart, and all the milk spilled out onto the street?"

(Meri was Aunt Chrisi's daughter.)

"No."

"And the driver came and demanded payment from Aunt Chrisi for all the milk."

"Did he get it?"

"How could he? We had no money back then. I don't understand how we got by. Some had a little more than others, but not like today, when people run around with wads of money in their pockets and still complain."

I recognize this bewilderment. It is the bewilderment of the poor when faced with those who don't know how fortunate they are. When I was a child I dreamed of a tricycle, which I never got. My children had gone through several bikes before they turned twelve. Not to mention my grandchildren. They still complain. In our district in Athens, we didn't even have a ball. We made one ourselves out of rags. It didn't bounce too well, but it was beautiful.

"I guess the world has progressed," I say.

My mother agrees, although she does have certain objections.

"We used to be hungry, now we're constipated. We used to be skinny, and now we're fat. We worked all hours, and now we sit around doing nothing. We loved our families, and now we love ourselves. It's lucky I'm so old! I can't cope with much more of this craziness."

I could argue with her, tell her that what she says isn't true. People work hard today too, they go hungry, they love their families. But I know she grieves for the world that has disappeared, and that this grief will not be cured by a sound argument.

So I say nothing. Watching your world fade away while you are still living in it isn't easy.

"Oh, my child! Soon you will be leaving again, and who will I talk to then?"

There are tears in her eyes.

"Mom, I only just got here," I say stupidly.

Maybe I would have said even more stupid things if the rain hadn't suddenly come down the way it can do in Athens. Within minutes the streets are transformed into raging rivers. The guttering on the balcony overflows, like a tired old heart that can't take any more.

My mother hurries indoors.

I STAY OUTSIDE, THE balcony is covered. The heavens open like a sluice gate and the water pours down. There is no beautiful Greek word for it. There is no particularly beautiful Swedish word for it either. But the French have a word:

l'orage. I learned it when I read Georges Simenon's Maigret books in French. At regular intervals Inspector Maigret was taken unawares by an *orage* and sought refuge in a café where he invariably ordered white wine.

You might of course wonder why I choose a French word. Is it because I am an old snob?

Maybe, but that's not the whole truth. The advantage of the French word is that Simenon tells us what time of year this kind of rain falls. It is a spring-summer rain. There is warmth in the air, the women are wearing thin skirts, the men are in open-necked shirts. Compare this with downpour—what does that make you think of?

Personally I think of the British bombers who swooped down from the sky one summer morning in 1941 and dropped their load on our village. They attacked in thunderous waves, over and over again, but their accuracy wasn't great. I was three years old, and I sat in the yard and watched them and I didn't get hit once.

That is the difference between *orage* and downpour. Am I an old snob, or just old?

I wait out *l'orage* on the balcony.

What would my life be without art and literature? What thoughts would I have in my head? I am remembering my Greek friend, who is my colleague in every respect. He is not only an author and an aging man, but he also writes in a different language from our own: in French. In one of his best books he writes that the main character sends his beloved an exquisite little perfume bottle that contains not perfume but rain from Paris where he sits alone, longing for her.

Every city has its rain. "The tears are falling in my heart as the rain is falling on the city," Verlaine wrote. However, I am not in Paris but on my mother's balcony in Athens, and it is indeed raining on the city but also on my head, as there are a number of holes in the awning. Plus I am getting hungry.

"I missed a shooting star because I had to tie my shoelaces," Rimbaud wrote. That's how it is. We miss the stars because we have to gather wood for the winter. We miss life because we always have to do something else. Didn't someone write that "life is somewhere else"?

My brain hops from one quotation to the next like a sparrow from branch to branch. I live my life surrounded by stories I haven't written, but I am grateful that others have. "Life goes before art," says Gombrowicz. He is right. Life goes before art, but it is art that emerges first.

And so it is time for my mother's artichokes à la polita, served up with the story of my maternal grandfather. He was the one who had taught her to make the dish, along with so many other things.

MY MATERNAL GRANDFATHER WAS called Stelios, and he was born in Egypt at some point during the 1880s. His father was a skipper from the notorious Peloponnesian area known as Mani, which thanks to its natural inaccessibility and the strategic abilities of its inhabitants when it came to war, was never conquered by the Turks, even though the rest of Greece formed part of the Sultan's empire. The people who lived there were seafarers and warriors, pirates and looters of wrecked ships, and some decided to move across the sea to the Egyptian coast, including my grandfather's father. He settled in Alexandria and eventually brought over his wife, who was also from Peloponnese. He commanded both his own ship and his wife, whom he made pregnant five times, but four of the children died young from various epidemics that swept through Africa at regular intervals.

My great-grandmother became desperate, terrified of losing her youngest son too. No one knows exactly what happened, but she left her husband in Egypt, taking her son with her, and came to live in our village, where she had inherited a considerable fortune from her parents. Did she rebel against her husband, or were they in agreement that she should try to save their son? We don't know.

When she arrived in the village, things went wrong from the outset. On the pretext that she needed a protector, her brother persuaded her to sign most of her fortune over to him.

What happened next has become a legend, both within our family and in the life of the village.

The two siblings had been to see the justice of the peace and signed the papers. When they came out, my great-grandmother allegedly said to her brother, "And now, dear brother, you can give me a piece of land so that I can build a house for myself and my son."

The brother, who had a severe speech impediment and an extremely nasal tone, slapped his elbow with the palm of his hand and replied, "This is all you're going to get, sister!"

My mother imitates both the speech impediment and the gesture, and laughs.

"Why the elbow?" I ask.

"Why the elbow? Because there is nothing on an elbow. Not even a single hair."

"What was her name?"

My mother looks at me, narrowing her eyes.

"What do you think, my Einstein?"

I daren't guess, for fear of saying something dumb.

"She was called Antonia, like me. Or rather Antonitsa. That's how it was back then. The grandchildren were given the paternal grandparents' names. If there were more than two children, then the maternal grandparents could be brought in. Your half brother was named Giorgios after his paternal grandfather, your brother is called Stelios after my father."

"I'm the only one who isn't named after someone," I complain.

"If you had been a girl, you would have been called Eleni, like your paternal grandmother. But you weren't a girl, you were a boy, and you disappeared to distant lands."

She notices that I am hurt. I didn't leave my country for fun, at least I don't think so, but I'm not entirely sure why I left.

"Don't worry, my son. I am only joking. I know why you left. There was nothing for you here. We couldn't give you anything."

Now she is the one who is sad.

"You gave me everything I am," I say with my mouth full of artichoke.

My words do not console her.

"Do you have any idea how many times I thank God that you went to Sweden, to those kind people who allowed you to study, gave you work, prizes, and medals? You became an author and lifted us up out of obscurity, as your father used to say. I sit here in the evenings and talk to your photograph. It is such a wonderful picture of you, it's as if you are sitting here opposite me. To think you're a grandfather! Soon you will be as old as me. Sweden was your salvation!"

The photograph she is talking about shows a young man, twenty-two or twenty-three years old. It is obviously me, but I don't recognize myself. Anyway, my mother likes talking to that photograph, which hangs on the wall beside her bed. On the wall opposite her is my brother. The whole apartment is full of photographs, old and new. On large tables and small tables, on the television set, on the refrigerator, on the dresser and the nightstand. She is surrounded by the dead and the living. I wonder if she talks to them too? I'm sure she does, because my mother has understood that words provide the greatest solace. What does she say to them?

"Anyway, you chose your name yourself. You were born on the feast of Saint Theodor. 'Wife,' your father said, 'the child has chosen his name.' There is always someone who breaks the chain. It was you, and you were the one who traveled far away, although you never took a step away from my skirts. Imagine if you had been a girl instead."

"Mom, you're the only woman I know who thinks that," I say in order to make her laugh, although it's not entirely true. I once met an Italian banker who was determined to come on to me.

The question of why I left home has never ceased to trouble me. I feel somehow guilty, as if I have shirked my responsibilities and am reminded of this fact on a daily basis. "You left here and saved yourself," I hear from both my family and other people. It is as if I have no right to express my views on Greek matters, because they no longer concern me. A gag is the first thing you get when you arrive in a new country, and a gag is the first thing you get when you return to your old country. "Life in a foreign country isn't for everyone," my mother sometimes says. Nothing is for everyone. I suddenly think about a story I heard a long time ago. "Daddy, is it far to America?" the boy asks. "Shut your mouth and keep swimming!" the father replies. That is the life of an immigrant.

My mother notices my silence, and continues with the tale of my great-grandmother. Even though her brother tricked her, she had enough money left to enable her to live comfortably and take care of her son, who grew up like a prince. He was good-looking, with blond hair and blue eyes, and many of the girls in the village saw him in their dreams. He wasn't the sharpest knife in the drawer when it came to school, but then he didn't need to be.

At the age of twenty he saw my maternal grandmother for the first time at a market. That same evening he told his mother, "It's her or no one." She wasn't happy.

My grandmother wasn't what you would call a catch. Her mother was a widow, there was no fortune, no prospect of a decent dowry. But what could my great-grandmother do? Faced with her son's determination, she gave in.

"There were people in the village who never forgot that wedding. There was never a more attractive couple," my mother says.

I only knew them when they were old and find this difficult to imagine. My grandmother always wore the same ankle-length black skirt. A thin body and a thin face, narrow lips, only a few teeth left.

"Grandmother was beautiful?" I say with some skepticism.

"As beautiful as a swallow."

Once again my mother is inside Greek mythology. She has no idea, but that doesn't matter.

Why is the swallow beautiful?

Because it hasn't always been a swallow. When the world began she was a lovely young girl called Heledon, who lived with her father the king of Miletus, the wealthy city on the west coast of the Mediterranean Sea. Her sister Aedon was happily married and lived in a different town with her husband, a skilled craftsman, and her only son. The couple incurred the displeasure of the gods because they boasted about their happiness. Shortly after that, they began to challenge each other over who was the best at what they did. The husband decided to build a chariot, the woman chose to weave a huge carpet. She won. The husband was crushed. He went to see his wife's sister and persuaded her to come back home with him for a visit. On the way he raped her, and threatened to kill her if she ever told her sister. Then he cut off her hair and gave her as a slave to his wife, who didn't recognize her. A while later, Heledon was sitting alone and weeping by the spring. Her sister recognized her, they fell into each other's arms, and the truth came out. Aedon was furious. She slaughtered her only son and fed the pieces of his dismembered body to her husband. Then she left with her sister for Miletus, where their father was king. A servant revealed to Aedon's husband what he had eaten. Enraged to the point of madness, he rode after his wife, but was captured by the king's men. They tied him to a tree, stripped him naked, and smeared his entire body with honey, then left him for the enjoyment of the ants and flies and wasps. Aedon couldn't bear to see her husband suffer and released him. This made her father and brother so angry that they wanted to kill her. It was time for the gods to intervene once more. They changed the entire family into birds. The husband became a pelican, the father a sea eagle, the brother a cockerel, Aedon a nightingale, and Heledon a swallow. She was also granted the privilege of living close to people because she had called upon Artemis, the goddess of chastity, at the moment of her rape.

So that is why my grandmother was as beautiful as a swallow, and this swallow gave birth to two children in quick succession, my uncle and my mother, at which point my grandfather decided it was time to try his luck in America, as so many others in the village had done before him.

"He went off and left us alone. He was gone for six years. We didn't hear from him very often. We received a few letters, but he could barely write and my mother couldn't read, so he stuck to the essentials. 'Dear wife, I am well. I hope you are too. America is good, but not for everyone. I will be back soon. I kiss you and the children.' I learned those letters by heart because my brother read them aloud to our mother. We heard from others that he traveled around from town to town. Sometimes he was a cook, sometimes a quarryman, sometimes a railroad worker. When he eventually returned he brought no money, but he did bring presents, mostly worthless items. He gave my mother a bell to ring when it was time to eat and a gramophone—the first in the whole county. My poor mother! My father was a good person, but his head was in the clouds. However, he had golden hands. Everything he did, he did well. Everything he planted flourished. Do you remember the lemon tree in the yard, or the fig tree? He planted those. And as time went by he earned plenty of money, but he lost it after the war. I'm not complaining. He was a good person. He never hurt a fly. Blessed be his soul!"

I actually remember a violent blow administered by him, but I don't say anything. It was meant for my brother, but my grandfather couldn't catch him, so he walloped me instead.

Speak of the devil—my brother suddenly arrives.

"Have you already eaten?" he asks.

I immediately remember my mother's advice.

"You're just in time. I've never tasted such artichokes—where did you buy them? God bless you!" I say.

He cannot hide his pleasure. His face lights up, but a second later he is back to normal.

"It was hell finding a parking space," he says.

My mother looks at us with satisfaction, like a director seeing her actors following their instructions to the letter.

Sometimes that's how little it takes to make people happy.

THE RAIN EASES BUT doesn't stop. My mother goes for a lie-down after we've eaten. Later in the afternoon my sister-in-law drops by. My brother calls to say that he isn't coming back "in this bloody awful weather." My nephew had said that he would phone, but he doesn't. However, my half brother's wife calls from Thessaloniki. She has a cold. I console her with the news that I have one too. I also speak to my half brother's son, who is a pharmacist and gives me good advice about my cold. Then his sister calls. She is a dentist and always cheerful. I also get to exchange a few words with her daughter, a talented sixteen-year-old who for some reason seems to like me. She expresses her devastation over that fact that I am in Greece but can't find the time to visit.

"Why, uncle? Aren't we people too?"

Faced with such an unanswerable question, all I can do is promise that I will definitely visit next time.

My brother phones at about eleven o'clock to tell me that one of my classmates, who had become an actor, is playing the lead role in a movie that is due to start on TV at any moment.

I think about it. I know he is a very good actor, but on this particular evening I prefer to remember him as a classmate.

Sometimes our memories also demand solidarity.

I CAN'T SLEEP. I am missing my Swedish family. At home in Huddinge I would frequently find myself standing in the hallway at a loss, not knowing where to go. I was waiting for my son to come down the stairs, nine years old and with his socks in his back pocket. Or for my daughter, aged six, to shout that there was a spider in the bathroom.

When I am home alone I often go and sit in their old rooms. There is still a sticker on the door that was first my son's and then my daughter's. "Better to ask and appear ignorant than to stay that way." I don't remember who put it up, or when. In my daughter's closet I found the special clothes she used to wear when she was training in karate and used to come home in the evenings covered in bruises, wanting me to fight her so that she could show off her skills.

In my son's cupboard I found his first tennis racket. He had talent, but at the age of fourteen he came home one night after training, took off his shoes, and showed me the soles of his feet—blisters everywhere. "I'm done with tennis, Dad," he said. He's never picked up a racket since.

I looked at my discoveries and smiled, then I got angry with myself. "It's time to come to terms with it," I said out loud, as if I were speaking to the neighbor. It's not impossible that that's exactly what I was doing. We ourselves are only our closest neighbors. The truth is I've never gotten used to the fact that the children are adults now, living their own lives.

My mother has the same problem. She can't escape her memories. She misses the grown man I have become less than the little boy I used to be.

It would be easy to say that both she and I miss our respective youths. However, I know that I don't miss myself as a young person. What am I supposed to miss? My fleshy nose? The febrile arrogance?

If there is one thing I do miss from my youth, it is the ecstatic joy of reading. What a treat, reading Dostoyevsky or Hamsun for the first time!

So it's not my youth I miss but my children when they were children. Is that so strange?

I miss them as adults too, but that carries no pain. They will be adults for as long as I live, but they were children only once.

It is long after midnight. I am lying on the sofa bed. There isn't a sound from my mother's room. I have no chance of falling asleep.

All I can do is return to my father. I had left him as a newly married hero, employed as a teacher in the district of Kontoskali in Constantinople. He was thirty years old.

THE THIRD DAY

At this time, immediately after the war, the teaching of the Turkish language became compulsory for the Greek schools and the other minorities' schools in Turkey.

I was entrusted with this task because I was the only one among my colleagues who spoke Turkish well. Eventually the principals of the minorities' schools had to learn Turkish. Some refused and were dismissed. I became the principal of a girls' school because my predecessor didn't speak Turkish.

In April 1924 our first child was born. A colleague stood as his godmother, and today when I write down these memories, she is still in Constantinople. The boy was given the name of my late father, Giorgios.

He was born with a swelling on his upper lip. He was a very beautiful fair-haired child with blue eyes, and he looked exactly like my father.

Unfortunately in October 1924 we were forced to leave our comfortable, pleasant life in Constantinople and move to Greece, in accordance with the Greek-Turkish Treaty of Lausanne, signed after the catastrophe in Asia Minor—by which I mean the Greek army's total defeat in 1921. This cruel and inhuman treaty required the Greeks in Turkey to be exchanged for the Turks in Greece. It didn't apply to Greeks who were born in Constantinople and registered there, but I was born in Trebizond and didn't have the right to stay.

And so in October 1924 I arrived in Piraeus with my family. During this period the Greek population left Turkey in large numbers in order to escape the manic thirst for vengeance with which freestanding Turkish factions known as Tjetes murdered every Greek, burned down their houses, and stole everything there was to steal. For that reason thousands and thousands of people gathered in Piraeus.

The hotels, the schools, the churches were overflowing with small children and ailing men and women. On the grounds of the Holy Trinity church, we put up a makeshift tent using our sheets and spent our first night there.

The next day one of my wife's uncles came and took us to his wooden barrack in the Kokkinia refugee camp in Piraeus. We stayed there for a week.

In the days that followed I visited the Education Department and was offered a post in the elementary school in Richea, a village high up on Mount Parnonas. I wasn't happy, but what choice did I have? We had to get out of the hell that was Piraeus at any price.

I accepted the job and we sailed from Piraeus on a specially chartered vessel, because there was no regular traffic on that route. On November 4, we reached Monemvasia. We spent the night in the local hotel that was owned by Kollias, who was famed for both his fish and his physical bulk.

Unfortunately some people with no conscience stole our belongings during the night. We had saved them from the Turks, and we lost them in Greece. In the morning we traveled by car to Molai with only the clothes we were wearing. Molai is a pretty town, the largest in the province.

There I met the mayor of Richea, Panagiotis Douros, who had lived in America for several years. He was comfortably off and progressive. He immediately showed great interest in us. He promised to send three bearers to fetch us the very next day, then he returned to Richea. That night we slept in the loft above a café, and in the morning the three bearers were waiting outside with their mules.

It was ten o'clock on November 5, 1924. We clambered onto the mules and after five hours of risky climbing, we arrived in the village feeling exhausted and dizzy.

Fortunately accommodation was provided for the school's employees; we were given a single-story house with a cellar, three bedrooms, and two kitchens. We moved in right away.

At first everything seemed difficult. Maria wept constantly. She was right to do so. She thought

this felt like an exile, and to be honest I have to say
that it was very hard for her to get used to living
in this mountainous region after all those years in
Constantinople, where she was born and grew up.

The nights were the worst part. Darkness
everywhere, thicker than tar. When the sun set,
everyone went home. The only sound was of barking
dogs and braying mules.

And how was she supposed to cook, bake
bread for the family? Everything seemed like an
insurmountable obstacle.

And yet we very quickly became accustomed to
our new life. The generous gifts of oil, cheese, eggs,
wood, soap, fruit, and vegetables from the hospitable
people of Richea worked miracles from the second
day. The tricky problem of provisions was solved
immediately.

The water supply was also an issue. Richea has
no running water. There are no rivers, just torrential
streams that dry up in the summer. People have
cisterns where they collect rainwater for all their needs
throughout the year. Every family has one, some have
two or three. There are also cisterns in the meadows
up on the mountain, where the animals graze.

The inhabitants were farmers, raising both crops
and animals. They had lots of olive trees, but widely
spread out rather than in groves. There were two
classes in the school, and the building was attractive.
In the first year a hundred and sixty-five pupils
were enrolled, boys and girls. Some children were

not enrolled; their parents preferred to have them tend the goats. While I was waiting for a colleague to be appointed, I started teaching on my own. Unfortunately no colleague arrived, and I toiled on alone. I worked ten hours a day in order to keep up. My wife helped out with the youngest children, and she also took on embroidery and other handicrafts.

Maria soon got to know the young girls in the village, who would often visit and ask her to teach them how to cook, sew, and embroider. She was overjoyed at this opportunity to be of use to these women, who lived far away from any kind of progress.

The work in school went wonderfully well, and the inspector who came to see us was full of enthusiasm. Everything had fallen into place for us. We were happy. Our child was growing normally. The nutritious food and fresh mountain air brought color to his cheeks. We were contented and always in good spirits. All the troubles and difficulties connected with our hasty departure were forgotten. Happiness and joy ruled in our home.

Alas! That happiness was very short-lived. A beautiful, fleeting dream.

I set the text aside. I know what is coming and can't face reading on. One thing is clear: My father was in love with Maria.

Was he ever in love with my mother, the ninety-two-year-old woman who is sleeping just a few feet away from me in the old double bed they shared for more than fifty years?

Was my mother ever in love with him?

I don't know. What I do know is that they had been loyal to each other and to us children to the best of their ability. My mother put it in her own way. "Your father never said to me, 'Move so I can get by.' And you children always came first. 'Antonia,' he would say, 'take care of the boys like your own eyes!'"

Maybe a marathon requires a different kind of dedication than a sprint. Maybe some people are sprinters while others are marathon runners. The tragedy is when a sprinter falls in love with a marathon runner, and vice versa. They will never run at the same pace.

Both of my parents appeared to be marathon runners. Each was certain that the other would never let them down. My father, who was much older, expected to die first, but he didn't need to worry that his son from his first marriage would be treated unfairly.

"I trust you, you have a good heart," he used to say to my mother. Presumably that wasn't all she needed, but it was all he could give her—and all she could give him.

It's important to remember how much that is.

It is after three o'clock. I should be able to manage a couple of hours' sleep before the doves get going.

I AM WOKEN BY the aroma of coffee. My mother is already up. I hear a sizzling sound from the kitchen as if she is frying something, and I know what it is: loukoumades. I look at the clock—after nine. It is a long time since I slept so late. Neither the doves nor the garbage truck had disturbed me. I must have been really tired, or else I have reverted to being a child.

Suddenly my mother is standing over my sofa bed carrying a cup of coffee on a tray.

"Did you sleep well, my treasure?"

I had, even though the sofa bed is rock-hard and the pillow even harder.

"You brought me coffee!"

I sit up and take the tray, and my mother sits down on the chair opposite without saying anything. She simply wants to see me drink her coffee.

The silence lasts a minute or so.

Is there anything in life that can replace or even come close to this? I think.

We are as close to each other in this ordinary, everyday moment as a stamp on a letter, and my mother is the letter writer.

This inactivity can't last forever, particularly as the loukoumades require her attention.

A few minutes later I am sitting on the balcony eating them, warm and dripping with honey. My mother takes only one, but I am pretty sure she has already eaten several in the kitchen. I can see it in her face. She looks like a cat who has just swallowed the fish from the aquarium. We have another cup of coffee.

"What are you going to do today?" she asks me.

The weather is beautiful.

"I might go for the walk I didn't do yesterday."

"You're like your father. He couldn't manage without his walks, and for many years he tried to get me to go along with him."

"He lived to over ninety as well."

"That was his revenge!"

This comes as a surprise. "I don't understand."

My mother leans forward as if she is about to reveal a secret.

"'Wife, they tricked me out of my compensation when I retired. Now I'm going to force them to pay my pension for another thirty years.' That's what he said to me. And you know what? I've done the same."

In Greece the widow inherits her husband's pension.

"Together your father and I forced this robbing state to pay us a pension for almost fifty years, and it's not done yet. I'm only ninety-two. What is the pension like in Sweden?"

I think for a moment. What is the pension like in Sweden?

I reached retirement age three years earlier, but I haven't taken my pension. I intend to work until I am seventy. I do a rough calculation in my head.

"It's enough to live on," I reply. "I'll get around a hundred and sixty euro more than you per month."

"No more than that, after forty years' work? Why don't you come out with it and say you're being exploited too?"

"We like it."

She laughs. "In that case everything is fine."

One thing definitely isn't fine. It is almost ten o'clock, and there is still no sign of my brother.

"Aren't you going to give him a call before you go out?"

I do exactly that. No reply.

"Where can he have gone at this early hour?" my mother asks.

I try to reassure her. "Maybe he's in the bathroom."

"Just like your late uncle Giannis in Molai. Do you remember him?"

Who could forget Uncle Giannis? He was one of the most well-established figures in the village, and constantly constipated. When he was sitting on the outside toilet he would have the church bell ringer stand outside reading aloud from twenty-year-old newspapers. According to Uncle Giannis, the news was repeated year after year. Names changed, different states were involved in war, people starved in different countries. But if you peeled away all of that, nothing remained except what Uncle Giannis referred to as "man's insanity." Along with the constipation, this was his biggest problem.

"Why do you care so much about the world?" the other villagers asked him.

"Who says I care about the world? I would shit on the world, if only I could," Uncle Giannis replied with a sigh.

On one occasion he came to visit us. My mother had prepared one of her "famous" kourambiedes—of which more later. Uncle Giannis ate it greedily, then muttered, "That slipped down very easily. Who knows when it will come out again."

No, I haven't forgotten Uncle Giannis.

"The people who were alive back then!" my mother goes on. "Each of them had their own craziness. Now everyone is crazy in the same way: money, money, money. That's all that matters. When I tell my friends that you are an author, they say, 'Oh? And how much a month does he earn?'"

"Speaking of which, how are your finances?"

She gazes at me, her expression serious.

"Your father left me like a princess. I have my home, I can give whatever presents I want to give to my grandchildren, and I have some money in the bank for my ticket."

"Your ticket?"

She shakes her head, irritated by my stupid question.

"For my final journey."

She says this with absolutely no undertones or overtones. She has lived long enough to catch up with death. It doesn't scare her. But it costs money to cross over. It always has. The ancient Greeks placed coins in the coffin so that the deceased would be able to pay death's ferryman.

Another example of how my mother lives within our mythology, in the belief that she is living in her reality. Once again I see how the story of death is stronger than death itself. Once again I see that my mother is my true country. If I were a piece of fruit, she would be the tree. If I were a tree, she would be the earth. If I were the earth, she would be my sky.

But at the moment I am none of these things, and my mother has more pressing concerns.

"I have to go in and make some loukoumades for your brother, when he arrives."

"You've always taken care of us," I say warmly.

It makes her happy, and she feels the need to boast a little.

"You call that taking care of someone? Do you remember that time we came to Italy to meet you?"

I nod. It was during the period of the junta, and I wasn't allowed to visit Greece.

"On the ship from Brindisi the Italians in the dining room gave me a round of applause."

"Why?"

"Because I peeled the skin off a peach before I gave it to your father. Those poor Italians! They had never seen anything like it. '*Quel figlia!*' they shouted, and the captain kissed my hand, but your father wasn't happy. 'They think you're my daughter,' he muttered, and I had to stand up and yell, '*No, no figlia! Donna!*' Your poor father! He didn't like the fact that I was so much younger, but I never thought about it. He was jealous too. And he wanted me close to him all the time. Sometimes, when I had a cold for example, I would go and lie down on the sofa bed. 'No, no, this is your place,' he would say, pointing to the space beside him in the double bed."

Here come the tears, I think, but I am wrong. She gives a brief laugh instead and hurries into the kitchen.

I feel the need to tease her.

"You didn't ask me what we should have for lunch," I call after her.

The response is like lightning.

"I have taken steps."

That shuts me up.

THE PREVIOUS DAY'S RAIN has worked miracles. The air is fresh and the sun feels as if it were brand new. In the square, the waiters are setting out tables and chairs. The smell of freshly baked bread spreads from the bakery. The stylish old barber brings his chair out onto the sidewalk, lights a cigarette, and watches the girls go by. The ladies' hairdresser opposite looks at herself in the mirror. Who knows what she sees.

I can't decide what to do: take a leisurely stroll in the park among the pensioners and mothers with small children, or wander around the local area in order to wave to my memories once more.

While waiting for inspiration to strike I keep on walking, and suddenly I feel as if an electric shock has passed through my body. I am standing outside Saint Eleftherios church. On my right is the elementary school that I attended for four years.

Admittedly a great deal had happened during that time, but nothing traumatic. I had arrived there as a boy from the country with the wrong clothes and the wrong dialect. I had received my fair share of derision from the other children, but within a short time I learned how to fit in, and the teacher, the unforgettable Magister Pavlou, was always on my side.

I often wonder what my life would have been like without these teachers. Magister Pavlou in the elementary school, who was the first to point out that I had been given a gift. He was always elegantly dressed, and each evening he took a walk with his beautiful wife. This short walk was his gift to the run-down district, the spouses side by side in perfect step, creating ripples of pleasure and quiet happiness around them. For a while we thought he was having an affair with the gymnastics teacher, but we could never be certain. Magister Pavlou always had a good word to say about my essays. He would read them aloud to the whole class. I had arrived as an outcast and he made me into a king.

Later, at the high school, I was blessed to have Giannis Raïsis as my Greek and Latin teacher. He got me to read the ancient Roman poets' love poems—that was my punishment for truanting, crushed by a broken heart. He made me understand what kind of gift I had been given, and what it meant. And my history teacher Elias Georgiou, who honored me by asking for my help. He had a doctorate in history and never stopped researching. I had to gather some information for him and take it to his home—a freezing-cold, unprepossessing apartment. He was sitting there writing, with gloves on. His desk was the only piece of furniture in the room. The rest of the space was taken up by gigantic rolls of newsprint. He noticed my confusion. "When I was in jail I missed paper more than anything," he said. I knew he had been imprisoned for his political views. "After that I swore I would never be without paper again," he added, with a touch of self-irony.

I have never forgotten the fire I saw burning in that freezing-cold apartment in Athens fifty-four years ago.

I was also saved by a couple of teachers in Sweden: senior lecturer Åke Löfgren and Professor Harald Ofstad, who both taught practical philosophy at the University of Stockholm and could see beyond the immigrant student's imbecilic and tortured use of language. Then there was Professor Marc Wogan in Uppsala, who agreed with incredible generosity to retest me for two grades in theoretical philosophy. I had already been failed three times in Stockholm—unjustly, in my opinion.

I give their names deliberately. Most of them are dead, but I will honor their memory for as long as I live.

Why are good teachers so undervalued these days?

So it isn't my old elementary school that has brought on the sudden panic, the feeling of not being able to breathe.

It is a window.

I have a long history with windows. It started at the age of three. One of my earliest memories is of sitting curled up by a window at home in Molai. In other words, it was 1941. A big war was going on, but it didn't exist for the child by the window, not even as a word.

What was I doing there? Who knows. Probably nothing. I curled myself around my life like the family cat who sometimes kept me company, with small signs of pleasure: purring when I stroked her, stretching her back, scratching her ears. Passersby saw us together and smiled.

It was peaceful. I can still remember those times today, above all the gentle pleasure of being indoors, as opposed to being outdoors. I didn't think in those terms, of course, but I was aware of the warmth from the stove, the sound of my mother's footsteps, and the voices of my older brothers, and it all combined to create the smile that I can see on my face, all these years later, in the yellowing photograph that my grandfather took.

It is the smile of a boy who hasn't been thrown out into the world but is enclosed by it. That smile disappeared and never returned when I left my country.

As pleasant as it was to be inside behind a window, it was equally painful to be outside. That meant merciless scrutiny. Pure fear was walking past the window where your beloved might be standing and watching you.

That is exactly what I do. I stand below Mary's window. By happy or unhappy chance, the building where she lived has survived. The surroundings have changed, of course. A blood-donor center has replaced the old stationery shop, but I could never have missed Mary's window. At the age of eleven or twelve I had been hopelessly and deeply in love with her. She was a wild tomboy with big green eyes, and she sang like an angel. She was also quite precocious, which meant that older boys were attracted to her too, so my love was doomed to failure from the start.

What did a twelve-year-old boy have to offer, compared with those well-built apes with hairy chests and legs? In the end one of them did indeed win her over. The idiot also had a motorbike. I never came to terms with it. Even though she had never hinted at anything, let alone made any promises, I regarded her decision as a huge betrayal.

The strange thing is that more than fifty-five years later, that same bitterness overwhelms me. Maybe bitterness isn't the best word in this context. It is more like an implicit sorrow, as if her betrayal wasn't a young girl's arbitrary choice but a proviso for my life—to be pushed aside, rejected, forgotten forever like one of those seriously mentally disabled children whose parents were so ashamed of them that they chained them up in dark cellars, with one small opening to give them food.

Such cases were often reported in the newspapers back then.

The pain of walking past her window after such a long time is just as acute as when I knew she was standing there with the blinds half drawn so that she could see me, my skinny shoulders, my bowlegs. Her gaze from behind the blinds made me hate my body and want to be someone else.

The idea that love helps us to become ourselves is a common delusion. In my experience, the reverse is true. Love forces us to want to be someone else. The beloved's gaze is our Procrustean bed. We don't fit, but instead of getting a new bed, we try to change ourselves.

(Perhaps I ought to explain for the reader who doesn't have access to a good encyclopedia that Procrustes was a mythical robber who compelled his victims to lie on an iron bed. If they were too long, he chopped off their legs and head. If they were too short, he stretched their legs and neck.

It was the Athenian hero Theseus who saved humanity from Procrustes. He defeated Procrustes in a fight, bent the trunks of two pine trees standing opposite each other, and tied one of Procrustes legs to each tree. Then he let them spring back to their original position and Procrustes was torn in half.)

It was Theseus who liberated us from Procrustes, but who will liberate us from love?

Mary's gaze behind the half-drawn blinds was my Procrustean bed. I don't know how many times I swore a sacred oath not to walk past that window again, only to do exactly that an hour or so later, over and over again. I didn't know at the time that you can never win someone's heart, however hard you try, and that sometimes you are given a heart without doing anything at all—or perhaps for that very reason.

It's true that I feel as if it had all happened only yesterday, but it wasn't yesterday. I am sixty-eight years old, and so is she. Would I recognize her if I saw her on the street?

Maybe, maybe not.

Why had I never contacted her during all these years? Why hadn't I made the slightest effort?

Possibly because these lines would be written one fine day.

Mysterious are the ways of the Lord, but the same can be said of his subjects, human beings.

The thought that she is old, that in the middle of playing with her grandchildren she might suddenly remember that skinny, bowlegged boy who adored her makes me feel calmer. Has she read any of my books? Does she ever regret rejecting me? Does she sometimes stand outside my window, shaking with resentment?

I can't possibly know that, and I don't want to know. Old wounds are useful. They make it easier to bear the new ones.

IT IS TIME TO turn to safer territory. The whole city has become a dead end. If I head toward the football stadium I will have to pass the former jails. Admittedly they have been torn down, but not inside my head. In there I am still haunted by images of the faces of the political prisoners behind the bars, which I had seen as a boy. For a while my half brother was in there too.

If I head toward the park I will be confronted by the place where a young woman, active within the resistance movement, was executed during the Nazi occupation.

In a few brief, apocalyptic moments the past springs to life. The violence, the poverty, the fear, the humiliation. I want to run. And where else would I run but back to my mom?

"Oh, Theo! You're such a baby in spite of your white hair!" I mumble in Swedish in an attempt to raise the Swedish words to form a strong wall between me and my city.

Oddly enough, it works. I feel calmer, I take myself off to a café and do what everyone else is doing on such a beautiful morning. Nothing. When you're drowning, you shouldn't panic and struggle, or you will be dragged down into the depths. You should lie still on your back, and hope that you float.

That is exactly what I am doing. For the first time after forty-two years in Sweden, there has come a moment in Athens, my city, when I can lie on my back on the sea of Swedish words—and I float.

Not for very long. I get up and set off again after a while. Just outside the funeral director's I stumble so badly that I crash headfirst onto the sidewalk. Immediately people gather around me. The funeral director comes rushing out too, and an elderly gentleman chases him away.

"He's not dead, for God's sake!"

I respond to their worried questions about how I am feeling, assure them I am fine, but they can see from my clothes and my pipe that I am not an ordinary Greek, and when it emerges that I live in Sweden, even more people gather to tell me they have been there, or have friends who've been there, or simply want to go there.

I answer all their questions to the best of my ability. Yes, we do have high taxes in Sweden. Yes, we do get a lot for our money. Yes, the women are beautiful. No, it wasn't the Swedish police who murdered Olof Palme or Anna Lindh. No, corporal punishment cannot be administered to children in Sweden. No, marital infidelity is not a crime. No, all Swedish men are not gay. In the end someone has had enough.

"Is there nothing wrong with Sweden?" he calls out.

"Yes, one thing. It's not Greece." I am ashamed of this demagogic reply, but I win a round of applause and am able to walk home with my head held high. And a slight limp.

MY MOTHER HAS DEFINITELY taken steps. When I walk in a good fifteen minutes before the agreed time, I am greeted by the unmistakable aroma of meatballs. It is embarrassing to admit that nothing comes close to my mother's meatballs, but it's the truth. She also has a spinach pie in the oven, which in no way resembles the ones you can get in Sweden, which are more like phantom pains. My mother builds up her pies with several layers of feta, rice, parsley, onions, and lots of olive oil. She ends up with a pie that melts in your mouth with a little crunch, a bit like fries but not as hard.

If you don't drink a couple of glasses of well-chilled retsina with all that you are either a barbarian or a wine expert—or both.

I praise her, which makes her happy, but she would be even happier if my brother were there. She saves some for him. Soon he will have quite a mountain to tackle, even though he is trying to lose weight. First the saved loukoumades, then the pie—and that is only the beginning.

My mother wants to know if I met any acquaintances on my walk.

"Only a few ghosts," I say.

Her expression grows serious. "You have no friends left."

"I do have friends, but it's so difficult to meet up with them. They have their families, their work, their commitments. I can't just call them up and say, 'Here I am, drop everything and meet me for a coffee.' I'm a stranger here, Mom, and I have to accept that."

"What about in Sweden? Do you have friends there?"

"They've thinned out recently."

I spoke only a week or so earlier at the memorial service for a departed friend, an immigrant like me but from Austria, a man who had left his mark on Swedish cultural policy. We had known each other for thirty years. In our younger days we sometimes played tennis or chess. As we grew older, it was just chess. I could see the loneliness growing around him, which had the peculiar effect of making him seek it more. In the end only a few old friends remained, along with a woman whom he loved. It doesn't sound like a small amount, but it was for him. He wanted to be a part of society, to have influence, to play a role. That was no longer possible.

More and more often he would say that he wanted to die. The first time we had a serious conversation about the matter was on the magical evening when Sweden beat Finland at football by a significant margin. We were sitting in the stadium at Råsunda shouting ourselves hoarse, and he wanted to die. I couldn't understand it.

He kept on losing weight and sounded increasingly tired on the phone, even though he was pleased when I called. In the end the condition I can only refer to as "resignation" took over. He lay down and waited for death. Every test you can think of showed that he was healthy, while at the same time he was mortally ill.

In his final days in the hospital at Danderyd it took a huge effort for him to speak. He ate nothing apart from the odd grape or cherry. But he smiled often.

On the very last day when I was about to leave, he suddenly spoke to me in German. I was so surprised that I couldn't believe my ears. Was he really speaking German?

"Are you speaking German to me?" I asked.

He smiled as if he were playing a trick on me. Then he said in German again: "*Vielen Dank für deinen Besuch.*" Many thanks for your visit.

A few hours later he was dead, but the last thing he had done was to return to his language, which he had almost fanatically avoided using during his whole time in Sweden, and which he claimed to have forgotten.

Someone within him remembered it. If a human being has a core, then it is this someone. And this someone is language, the first narrative.

"You're very quiet," my mother says, a little worried.

I look at her. The gray hair, the finely chiseled mouth, the lively brown eyes. Full of life, close to laughter and tears, sometimes for the same reason.

I feel such a deep gratitude that I have her here opposite me, warm and living. The thought that she will one day be gone is so distant and alien that it makes me remember what I believed as a child: that the tree outlives its fruit. But if I died first, how would she cope with such pain?

It is a circular argument that leads to only one sensible conclusion. We have a duty to remain immortal for each other.

"I'm so full I can hardly speak," I say.

My mother laughs, mightily relieved.

HOWEVER, IN THE AFTERNOON I come to my senses and call Diagoras. We had gotten to know each other in our first year of high school. We were thirteen years old. Shortly afterward we were joined by Giannis, who was in the same class. We were very different from one another, yet very alike. Diagoras thought the most, Giannis wanted the most and already knew he was going to be an actor. I read the most.

The three of us together did everything that boys of that age do. We confided in one another about everything, we played truant from school, we sneaked away from home and took the bus to the sea. Giannis was a magnet for girls, although he didn't know it. Diagoras was already a very deliberate seducer. Unfortunately I was neither one nor the other; I was usually unhappily in love and wrote poems.

When we graduated from high school, Giannis applied to a drama school and needed someone to read lines opposite him. Diagoras and I stepped up. All three of us went to the audition, and Giannis was brilliant. The funny thing was that we, his partners in crime, were judged to be not too bad and got in as well.

It was a fantastic time in my life. We met a drama teacher who set our famished souls on fire. Ibsen, Strindberg, Tennessee Williams, Eugene O'Neill, Arthur Miller, Bertolt Brecht, Ionesco, Jean Genet were just some of the completely new names to which he opened our astonished eyes, just as a street trader opens up ripe figs to show the customer that there are no grubs inside.

It was a party. We studied together, we played opposite one another, we had fun together. Giannis made his debut in Tennessee Williams's *Sweet Bird of Youth* at the age of only nineteen, and his costar was a goddess: Melina Mercouri. We were so proud of him, so proud.

We still are, forty years later.

Things didn't go too badly for Diagoras either. Over time he became a highly respected director, and led both the National Theater of Greece and the Greek Film Center at different times.

I was less successful. I left the country—but eventually everything worked out for me too.

We have met up only sporadically since those days, but the old glow is still there whenever we do get together.

It's a miracle!

But how long does a miracle last?

I have to admit to feeling a little nervous when I call Diagoras. I haven't seen him for a few years. My anxiety is unfounded—he is delighted to hear from me and immediately suggests calling Giannis.

We arrange to meet that very afternoon at the same café as before—Café Sonia, which like us has survived all these years.

I head over there with light footsteps, but find the café closed. Only temporarily though, for renovations. A few minutes later Diagoras appears, with his mustache à la Nietzsche.

"What the hell? It was open just few days ago."

I immediately realize that the miracle of our elderly friendship is still alive. He has immediately addressed the situation, without wasting a second on greetings or small talk.

Fortunately there is another café next door. It isn't Sonia, but it's okay. We call Giannis on his cell and redirect him. He is late and blames parking difficulties. He doesn't bother with welcome phrases either but points out that my hair is now completely white.

There is a ripple of excitement in the café because of his presence, but he handles it very calmly.

Diagoras asks about Swedish dramatists. I mention a few names and it turns out that he knows of them. He is looking for plays in his capacity as director of the theater whose drama school the three of us had once attended. This information makes me laugh out loud with joy. It isn't only the earth that is round—life is too. At least sometimes.

We sat here once a long time ago, dreaming. Now we are sitting here again after having achieved what we wanted to do, all three of us. An actor, a director, an author. That doesn't mean we lacked nothing. Diagoras regrets the fact that he has never given himself wholeheartedly to one thing. Giannis is worried about a strange pain in his stomach. I know the good books are behind me rather than ahead of me.

Once upon a time we sat here burning, and now we choose a table close to the fire to keep warm. However, we don't talk about memories but go straight for the present. It is as if we have continued to meet up on a regular basis and quickly fall into our former roles, which become crystal clear when it comes to paying.

When I ask for the bill, it transpires that Diagoras has already taken care of it. Somehow he has always been the Boss.

We part without any drama, as if we are going to see one another the following day. We had started in the same way, as if we had seen one another the previous day.

I must tell my grandchildren about this, I think. Aristotle, the wisest of the wise ancient Greeks, was right when he wrote that nothing is more precious than a friend.

WHEN I GET HOME I find my mother lying on the bed with my book in her hands.

"How's it going, Mom?"

She gives me a slightly embarrassed smile. "It's so heavy."

A stab of disappointment pierces my heart, but I keep the mask in place.

"Is it hard to read?"

"No, not at all. It's just heavy... holding it up like this... my arms are aching... I can't go on much longer, my son. Why are all books so thick these days?"

It is an important question. How can I possibly answer it?

"Giannis and Diagoras send their love," I say instead.

She puts down the book with palpable relief and asks lots of questions about my friends and their families. Finally she quotes Aristotle, without realizing it.

"Nothing is as valuable as old friends."

She knows what she is talking about. She has lived for so many years that she no longer has any left.

We share a quiet dinner, then we flick through the TV stations. Scantily dressed women, quizzes, old war movies. Nothing worth watching.

Fortunately it is almost time for the news, which is dominated by a collision between a Turkish and a Greek military aircraft over the Aegean Sea. The Turkish pilot managed to eject and was rescued by Greek fishing boats that hurried to the area. The Greek pilot wasn't so lucky, and hasn't been found.

"What do these Turks actually want?" my mother asks with a sigh.

For decade after decade Greek governments had fostered the Greeks' fear of their neighbors: Bulgarians, Turks, and Albanians. Then there were the Americans who made the decision and the British who did their best. The Greeks regarded themselves as a beleaguered people.

"Thank goodness the EU exists, otherwise we'd be at war all the time," my mother says after a while.

Like most of those who had experienced a war, it was the thing she feared more than anything.

"I'm not afraid for myself. I'm old, I have lived my life, but I am thinking of that young man's mother. Her child, her flesh and blood is gone. Such a big sky, and yet there wasn't room for those two boys. I don't know what to say. Has God grown tired of us?"

She is genuinely upset. I want to comfort her.

"It was an accident. Accidents happen."

"That poor woman!"

We switch off the TV and sit in silence for a while. It is almost eleven thirty. I think my mother looks as if she wants to sleep. I am wrong.

"You must make allowances for me, my boy. My eyes have seen so much. When I sit here alone at night, I think about everything we've been through. It is a miracle that we survived. It is a miracle that I survived, alone with three children and the Germans in the house."

"What are you talking about?"

"Don't you remember? We had four officers living with us. No, you were too little. A sweet blond boy that everyone spoiled. Do you remember Mario, the Italian? 'Bello bambino,' he said, and gave you candy. But the Germans left me in peace. 'Eine gute Frau,' they said, and they never even raised their voices to me. They spent all day wearing shorts, but in the evenings when they came home they would put on their long pants and ask my permission to play a few records on the gramophone my father had brought from America. You would stand to attention and salute them like a soldier, which made them laugh. No, I wasn't afraid of the Germans. And when they took your father and I wept, the German captain reassured me, told me nothing would happen to him. Your father had a fever, he was having one of his malaria attacks, and when they came to the river the water was rushing along and one of the Germans took your father on his back and carried him across to the other side. But our own wolves—Fascists and collaborators—I was terrified of them. They slaughtered people like goats. And I was on my own, twenty-seven years old, with three children. They didn't touch me either—I have my brother to thank for that. He was loyal to the king, and they respected him."

The depressing truth is that I have no recollection of any of this. I vaguely recall a soldier who gave me chocolate; I thought he was German, and his name was Franz. We cannot trust our memories. So how can we rely on the memories of others?

As time goes by our whole life becomes nothing more than a memory. If we can't rely on that, how can we know that we have lived?

I am very happy to hear that the Germans were kind to my mother.

"There are good people everywhere," she goes on. "Some folk are surprised that rosebushes have thorns, instead of thanking the creator for the fact that they have flowers. But it is the roses that are the miracle, not the thorns."

This could be said in several different ways, but probably not in a better way.

"Bravo, Mom! You should have been a writer instead of me."

She narrows her eyes.

"Do you think I don't have a brain, just because I didn't go to school?"

"And why didn't you?"

"Times were different then. I went to the elementary school for six years, but when I was due to go to the high school, that was the end of that. My mother wanted me to continue, and so did I, but both my father and my brother were against it. 'You're needed at home,' they said. 'What do you want to be? A nurse, wiping people's backsides? Or an unmarried teacher in some godforsaken dump?' They weren't wrong, to be honest. A woman didn't have many other options in those days. And I didn't have the courage to go against their wishes. It wasn't like it is now, when children have rights. Then it was only the sons who had rights. The girls were seen not as children but as servants. My own father pulled a face when I was born, because he had been hoping for another son. My maternal grandmother, who was a midwife, told me that.

"I remember when our Gunilla first came here with Markus. He was only two years old, but she sat and talked to him for hours when he refused to do what she wanted. No slapped legs, no pinching, no yelling. She simply sat and talked to a two-year-old!"

Gunilla is my wife and Markus our son. She brought him to Athens on her own so that my parents could meet him. I wasn't able to accompany them due to the generals' dictatorship in my country. They were ousted from power the following year, but the situation at home with argumentative children didn't exactly improve as our daughter, Johanna, grew up. She was, if possible, even more articulate, and extremely conscious of her rights.

"I wouldn't dream of raising a hand to my children," I say.

"Raising a hand? That's the least of it. I still remember and shudder over the way a father in the village killed his daughter."

"Who was it?"

"No names."

"Why did he do it?"

"Because there was a rumor that she had gotten together with her second cousin. She was seventeen years old. She was sitting barefoot, weaving, when along comes her dear father, pretending to be in a good mood and joking with his daughter. He tells her to put on her shoes because they are going for a walk, he wants to show her a field he has bought for her dowry. She didn't suspect a thing, although she did wonder why he was carrying his shotgun.

"'What are you going to do with the gun, Father?' the ill-fated daughter asked, and he lied, told her he'd seen rabbits earlier in the day. When they reached Monodentri—do you remember Monodentri? That ravine, with only a single tree growing? He shot her there, then went looking for the cousin, but he had left and never returned. That's how it was back then. Another strangled his daughter because she was pregnant by a married man. Then he threw her in the pool and claimed that she'd drowned. Your grandfather was a gendarme at the time, and he was there when the doctor examined the body.

"'She wasn't alive when she was thrown in,' the doctor said.

"'How can you be sure?' the captain of the gendarmes asked him.

"'Throw a live chicken and one that's been strangled into the pool and you'll see the difference,' was all he said."

"Yes, but what happened then? No trial, nothing?" I ask.

"I expect something did happen, but what does that matter? The girls were gone, their poor mothers wept pitch-black tears for as long as they lived."

She falls silent for a few seconds, as if she is giving herself time to recover.

"Oh my son, you make me remember so much."

Is that a complaint? It isn't, but she is too tired for any more.

The clock has struck twelve. The building is silent.

My mother sits here like this night after night, I think. *Okay, so my sister-in-law, my nephew, and of course my brother come to visit her, but eventually they have to go home, and my mother is left here with the whole night before her. And I am in Huddinge playing chess against my computer.*

Suddenly my betrayal is horribly clear to me, but I console myself with the thought that even if I had stayed, I too would have gone back to my own home in the end.

"Time you went to bed," my mother says. "I'm sure all my chatter has given you a headache."

I don't have a headache, but my soul is sore.

"Shall I turn out the light?" I ask.

"Yes please."

I do that, but the night-light in front of the icon and the wedding wreath still shines brightly.

"Shall I switch that one off too?"

"No, not that one."

It is just like when I used to put my children to bed. They both wanted a light left on, and so does my mother.

"Good night, Mom."

"Good night, my boy. And don't start reading now. Rest your eyes."

That isn't what she means. She just doesn't want me to disappear into some book, but she doesn't need to say that.

I already know.

THE FOURTH DAY

IT IS JUST SEVEN o'clock when the phone rings.

"Oh, it's market day," my mother says.

Of course it is my brother, calling to ask her what she wants him to buy. When she has finished, she hands the phone to me.

"Do you want to come along?" he asks.

"Absolutely. When?"

"Now. I'll be there in ten minutes. Come down so I don't have to search for a parking space."

"Okay."

We end the call.

"Your brother runs off to the market in the middle of the night. What is he afraid of? That they'll run out of cauliflowers?"

I don't respond because I am in a hurry. I know my brother. In ten minutes he will be at the door with his engine running. The street outside my mother's apartment building is narrow, and one-way. I quickly get dressed, brush my top teeth for the sake of my smile, and open the door.

"Are you going out like that?"

"What's wrong with me?"

"How much detail do you want? Your shirt is creased, jeans are for young men, your sneakers are too ugly, and you haven't combed your hair!"

"I don't have time. I'm not going to parliament—I'm only going to the market."

"Your late father never left the house without cleaning his shoes first, even when he was going to the market."

This is what the philosophers call "a necessary and sufficient argument." I do as she wishes with regard to my hair and my footwear, then I race downstairs and step out through the door at the exact moment when my brother's green car appears—green because like me he follows Panathinaikos, whose emblem is the green three-leafed clover. He too has an opinion on my appearance.

"Are you on your way to the gym?" he asks.

He is impeccably dressed in a matching shirt, pants, and light walking shoes.

"Don't you start as well," I say, but without conviction. I realize that this isn't about vanity but is a deep, culturally rooted desire to please one's fellow human beings. During the course of my life I had allowed myself certain liberties which, as a young man, I had regarded as proof of my independence. But the fact that my father always cleaned his shoes before he went out and that my brother was smartly dressed was not evidence of their lack of independence. It showed that they wanted to be a person among their fellow human beings, while I wanted to be *the* person. They honored others, while I honored myself.

You could of course say that they were collectivists suffering from a lack of freedom, while I was a free individualist. It's the same old problem that every society has to solve: shared obligations or individual freedom. Different societies deal with the issue in different ways, and they are characterized by the solutions they choose. In Sweden it is clear that shared obligations, with the sole exception of taxes, have been pushed aside, while individual freedom keeps on growing.

Why else has Stockholm become one of the filthiest cities in Europe? How come people urinate everywhere, drop trash in the streets and squares, yell when they talk to each other, and laugh like crazed gorillas in restaurants? How come students are allowed to take their cell phones into the classroom and use them?

In Sweden we tend to solve all social problems in one of two ways: through either higher taxes or greater personal freedom. In general we go further than anyone else in every direction at the same time. God help us!

How did things end up like this? I don't know. In the past I thought that only education keeps a society within the framework of common sense. Unfortunately, Hitler's Germany proved the opposite.

Perhaps we are victims of a merciless capitalism that has every reason to knock out any pockets of resistance within society, while transforming people from fellow citizens to clients. We no longer have relationships with each other but have transactions instead. Once upon a time the Catholic Church gave absolution in return for payment. Perhaps that will happen again. We'll get love checks with divorce as interest. The problem is not only that everything is for sale but also that everything is bought.

My brother misinterprets my silence.

"Don't sulk, I was only joking. Did you sleep well?"

"Like a donkey. And you?"

"Praise be those little pills. Check out the idiot behind us!"

"Can't you sleep without them?"

"Not for the last twenty years. Come on, granddad! That's why cars have a gas pedal!"

"Sleep is a problem too."

"My problem isn't serious. Don't you remember our brother, who never slept for more than an hour at a time? Oh dear oh dear! Here comes a wanker—and not just any wanker. Look at him!"

This is what it's like, being in a car with my brother. He conducts a constant dialogue with his fellow drivers, who seem to be unaware of it, thank God.

Indeed I did remember that our older brother never slept for more than an hour at a time. It was after he had been sentenced to death twice by a military court during the civil war. His crime? He had refused to rape two partisan girls who had been captured, defying his captain's orders. The entire company had done it before him, but he refused. Where do you find such strength?

I asked him once, long after the war.

"How did you find the courage to say no? The captain could have executed you on the spot."

"What would our father have said if I'd done it?"

That was his answer.

That's what it means to have a father. And a brother. He's dead now. He woke up one morning, made himself a cup of coffee, sat down on the sofa, and never got up again. An artery burst, and he was gone before he had time to drink his last cup.

"My father died as he had lived: discreetly," his son said.

And so one of the people I was proudest of disappeared. A kind, well-meaning, highly responsible man who smiled when he was thinking, and he spent most of his time thinking because he slept so little. He also laughed often, particularly when he was with my other brother. They couldn't look each other in the eye without bursting out laughing.

I will never see them like that again. Now I search my living brother's eyes for my dead brother's laughter.

He was one aspect of our father. My full brother represents another aspect, and he is aware of that. We arrive at the market, which is already in full swing in spite of the early hour. Vegetables, fruit, fish, nuts, cheeses, sweet treats, bread, and cookies are laid out on stall after stall. It is the kind of scene that always features in American movies when the two young lovers visit Italy for the first time.

We are neither young nor in love. I panic. My first impulse is to buy everything my mother has ordered as quickly as possible and get out of there. The traders are calling out their wares in loud, hoarse voices. Middle-aged men and women, mainly women, jostle in front of the stalls, constantly arguing over the quality and the prices.

"Those fish don't look too bad," I say.

"They've been frozen," my brother replies after a quick glance.

"How can you possibly know that?"

He ignores my question, with its insulting insinuation.

A while later he finds the fish he wants to buy. The stallholder isn't there, but no more than ten seconds later he appears. Short and squat, with gray hair, and wearing a wool sweater in the heat.

"Good morning boys. What can I do for you?"

"We wanted to see you," my brother comes back like lightning to put him off-balance, but it doesn't last long.

"I can show you more if you like," the guy says, pretending to pull down his pants.

Everything is mutually agreed. This is pure theater, even if the main roles are taken by several dead fish.

With the same X-ray vision my brother continues to choose between the thousands of items on sale, which to me look absolutely identical. How can he see a difference between this spinach and that? He is concentrating hard, going slowly from one stall to the next with me acting as his porter.

"Where did you learn to shop like that?"

My brother isn't one of those modern men who share the housework. He was born with a certain inclination to make the decisions, which his thirty-five years as a teacher had only served to intensify. On one occasion when his wife put down the ashtray three feet away from him, he asked her if he was supposed to take a cab to stub out his cigarette. However, after he retired he became a real homebody, much to his own surprise and everyone else's.

"The old man taught me."

The old man was our father.

He goes on: "I think about it sometimes. Our older brother had inherited the old man's morals, I inherited his sharp eyes and you his thirst for knowledge. It takes three of us to make a man like him."

"The two of us must have inherited something from Mom too."

"Absolutely—her sense of humor. The old man was very serious. He rarely laughed."

"But he smiled often."

"Our older brother had a sense of humor too."

"I can't believe he's dead. The two of you had so much fun at my expense," I say.

"You were actually pretty dumb when you were a kid. For one thing you couldn't talk properly and for another you believed everything anyone told you. Do you remember when I got you to race the cat?"

"Did I ever win?"

He laughs.

More and more people are arriving at the market. The tempo increases. People shop as if they are about to board Noah's ark, while we are already done. I am carrying five bags, he is carrying his wallet. But he had stayed put, and he called our mother at seven in the morning so that he could go shopping for her.

There is a kind of justice in this world, whether we like it or not.

———

OUR MOTHER IS WAITING for us.

"Welcome, my cypresses," she says.

That is an exaggeration. Over the years my brother has acquired something of a belly, and I have a vulture's neck thanks to all the time I have spent staring at a blank page.

My brother puts the shopping away, while I go out onto the balcony and light my pipe.

My mother hasn't been idle while we were out. A fresh batch of loukoumades is ready and waiting. She folds her arms and watches us as we eat.

"You have golden hands, Mom," my brother says, with his mouth full and honey trickling down his chin.

There we sit—he is seventy-four, I am sixty-eight, and our mother is ninety-two. The city around us is more than three thousand years old.

Life is not a dream.

Sometimes it's better than that.

When our mother goes to her room for a little while, my brother leans forward and whispers with a wry smile, "She's got us exactly where she wants us now."

"She's always been like that."

"A real dictator."

"Absolutely."

"It's fantastic that she's still with us. Her brain is as sharp as a razor. May we age like her, by the grace of God."

I remain silent for a moment. I want to say something, but it is difficult. I take a deep breath.

"I don't know if I've said this before, but I want to say it now. I am eternally grateful that you take care of Mom the way you do."

He looks at me with genuine astonishment.

"She's our mother. And the older she gets, the more I like her. I like old people in general. They have everything I lack. Peace of mind and body, they are genuinely pleased if you fetch them a glass of water. Although we do argue sometimes—especially about politics, she hates the privileges politicians have. 'Are they governing the country or eating it up?' she says. 'Every idiot drives a Mercedes. Where did they find them? In Grandfather's vineyards?' Then there are the moral issues. She hates divorce, short skirts, low-cut tops. As soon as some half-naked woman appears on TV, she changes to another station. 'Please Mom, let me see a little ass,' I say just to tease her. 'Haven't you seen enough?' she replies. Try it one evening, you'll see."

"We have to try to understand her. She has been on a long journey. During her life the world has changed several times. She needs something to hang on to," I say. "It's a miracle that these people didn't explode from the inside like pomegranates. They had to learn to live with so many new things, even though most of them were illiterate. I myself am turning into a conservative idiot as I get older," I add.

At that point my mother comes back. She has combed her hair neatly and is carrying a small bottle. It is her eau de cologne. She tips a few drops into the palm of her hand, rubs her hands together, then pats us on the cheeks—first my brother, then me.

"There—now you smell like me," she informs us.

We look at each other and say nothing.

At my mother's insistence my brother stays for lunch. After all, he has chosen the fish, and he has done an excellent job. They smell exactly the way fish should smell. My mother has fried them in lots of olive oil until they are crispy and golden brown, so that the skin actually tastes better than the flesh. She also serves feta cheese and boiled zucchini, with plenty of lemon and even more olive oil.

She praises my brother for his purchases.

"Bravo, Stelios—such wonderful fish!"

As if he had caught them himself.

He praises her for her skills with the frying pan, I praise them both, commenting with a slightly sour edge that I haven't contributed anything.

They protest immediately.

"You took a four-hour flight to come and visit us—how can you say that?"

In the end we are all happy, and we become even happier when it is agreed that I will take them out for dinner one evening.

"I'm sure you know a good place," I say ironically to my brother; he is always boasting about his friends and acquaintances, and what excellent service he gets. He looks at me to see if I am being ironic, realizes that I am, and laughs.

"My kid brother is teasing me," he explains to Mom.

"You were worse," she says. "You locked your great-grandmother in the outside toilet and refused to let her out. You climbed up onto the roof of our house so we couldn't catch you. You were a real little Beelzebub. Do you remember Mrs. Panagiota who had a brother in America? He sent over some candy, which she shared among her grandchildren. She didn't give you any, and you immediately insulted her. 'Why should I call you Mrs. Panagiota?'"

"I remember that," my brother says to my surprise. He seems to recall his childhood from the age of two with great clarity.

"Then there was the time you were given a little wooden car, which Grandfather had carved for you, and do you know what he did?" my mother goes on, turning to me. "He put it in the middle of the road and let the bus crash into it, to see if it would survive."

I want to say that my brother was getting things wrong even when he was a kid, as revenge for him saying that I was pretty dumb when I was a kid, but I keep quiet.

The conversation continues for a while longer, then my brother goes home. My mother decides to have a lie-down after washing the dishes. Once again I offered, and once again I was sent out of the kitchen.

"As long as I am on my feet, I will do my job."

It is so straightforward to her. I don't think that at the age of ninety-two she should have to wash the dishes after us, but she is proud that she can still do it at ninety-two.

"I hope that God will let me go standing upright," she adds.

That's how it is, I think later when I am lying on the sofa bed.

"There are those who die at their post, and those who die while being guarded."

You can retire from a job, but how do you retire from being a person among other people?

She washes up quickly and quietly, then goes to her room for a rest—but not before asking me if I would like a cup of coffee.

"No thanks. I think I'll have a sleep."

"Good idea. Sleep makes the baby stronger and the sun makes the wheat stronger, as my grandmother used to say."

"I remember I wasn't allowed to go to her funeral. She lived to a very old age, didn't she?"

"Yes—over ninety-five at least. Back then hardly anybody knew when they were born."

"Do you know when you were born?"

"The year and the month, but not the day. I'm told it was raining." She turns to go, then says, "Oh, my boy! If you only knew how happy I am that you are here, and when I think that you will soon be leaving again…"

Her eyes fill with tears, and she can't go on.

I don't say anything. I know how she feels. You spend the first few days realizing you're home—and the rest realizing you have to leave. Although it wasn't quite so simple in my case. Stockholm was also my home, even if my everyday life didn't have the opiate ease of Greek life. The truth was that I had already begun to long for my family, for the few friends I had, for Medborgarplatsen at eight o'clock in the morning when the florist is setting out cheap Polish roses, my study, the daily newspapers, Persson and Reinfeldt in a political debate on TV. I longed for expressions like "in peace and quiet" or "no idea," Kajsa Bergqvist beating herself up before she jumps, and Henke Larsson and Zlatan, who always prefaces a positive answer by saying "no" first.

I could say a great deal, but instead I say nothing.

———

IN THE AFTERNOON WHEN we are sitting on the balcony drinking coffee, my Greek publisher calls to tell me that the daily paper *Ta Nea* has reviewed my recently published book, the Greek version of *I hennes blick* [In her eyes]. I have a strong emotional relationship with the paper; my father had read it, and so had I for as long as I remained in the country. It had always had the best cultural section.

"Was I slaughtered?"

"Go and buy a copy, then you'll see."

That doesn't sound too bad.

It definitely wasn't too bad. It was fantastic. A whole page, with a picture too. The reviewer praised the book for everything it had been criticized for in Sweden. I didn't draw the conclusion that they were wrong in Sweden and right in Greece, which would have been easy to do.

I drew the conclusion that has become so controversial in recent times: that there are cultural differences, and that I had to live with them and try to circumvent them when necessary.

Greece has given fifty-two thousand words to the world, according to a sign at the Athens airport. Sweden has given the world the wrench, the creamer, the gear wheel, and the zipper. Imagine if I could set up a new world with the help of those Greek words and Swedish tools?

I like the idea.

My mother is pleased about the article too. I read selected extracts aloud to her.

She claps her hands.

"Goodness me, what a child I have given birth to!"

I can't work out whether she is making fun of me or the newspaper or both of us.

My son often used to complain that I didn't always take him seriously. His explanation was that it was difficult to take someone seriously when you had changed their diapers.

I often complained that my daughter didn't take me seriously, and she explained to me that you can take a lot of things seriously in this world, but not your father.

By whom should we be taken seriously, and when?

Believe it or not, this is one of the biggest cultural differences. In Sweden, lacking a sense of humor is regarded as a serious matter, while in Greece, lacking seriousness is regarded as humor. In Sweden there is too little irony, in Greece too much. I have to write my books somewhere in between, and live my life with my vulture's neck.

"It's not always that easy, Mom," I say, as if she knows what I am talking about.

Maybe she does, because she replies immediately: "I know, my child, but it's okay!"

The rest of the day is uneventful. I go for a walk and try to find the places where my childhood friends lived; all but one are gone. And even that is being demolished. I stand for a long time watching the bulldozers. One of the strangest young men in the whole city lived there. He was reading Nietzsche when the rest of us were indulging in competitive jerking off. As time went by he became a publisher and published the books he thought the Greeks ought to read. Then an insurance salesman paid him a visit in his modest office. "Why do I need another insurance policy?"

our friend asked. "You might have a break-in one of these days," the salesman pointed out. "If someone breaks in and steals the books, then at least he can't blame me," the young publisher replied.

There, in the building that is being reduced to rubble, he lived alone with his mother and nourished the dream of a different Greece. I have no idea what he is doing nowadays, but he must be disappointed. Our country is not what we thought it was, and it never became the country we had hoped for.

Or maybe we weren't the people we thought we were, and we never became the people we hoped we would be. Certainly not me. I had left that battlefield long ago. I had stopped blaming myself for doing so, but that doesn't mean I had forgiven myself.

They say that the perpetrator always returns to the scene of the crime. A reasonable, if somewhat optimistic, explanation could be the hope of undoing what had been done.

Why else did I keep returning to the scene of my crime? Not only in the physical sense but also spiritually. Only at the age of fifty did I start writing my books in Greek too. It wasn't a question of translation, it became clear quite quickly that I couldn't translate myself. I also wanted to be a Greek author, I wanted to come back and compete on the same terms, although in fact the terms would never be the same again.

That was of minor importance. The key thing was to return to my second great love: my Greek language, which is bigger than the world. But also to return to my first love, to the person who is that language and that world, and who sat alone in the evenings talking to my photograph instead of talking to me.

I think of Albert Camus, who was once asked if he would sacrifice his mother for the Cause, whatever it might have been, and he replied without hesitation that he would rather sacrifice the Cause for his mother.

That's how simple it was for him.

That's how simple it ought to be for me.

WHEN I GET BACK home I find my mother in front of the TV, watching a Greek series which for purely financial reasons had been shot in the summer. Needless to say, the women are scantily clad.

She immediately reaches for the remote to switch it off.

"Please, Mom, let me see a little ass," I say, just as my brother had urged me to do.

She hesitates for a couple of seconds, looking at me to check if I am bluffing. She makes her decision.

"Okay, as you'll be leaving soon."

In other words I, who had left, have certain privileges that are not afforded to my brother, who had stayed.

There is a kind of justice in everything. And an injustice.

THE FIFTH DAY

I WAKE UP HAPPY. The hard sofa bed feels soft, the sounds from the backyard are like a harmonious expression of a good life, the clattering and banging in the stairwell form a discreet general bass.

It is a little after six o'clock. I have no other plans for the day apart from trying to finish my father's narrative.

Therefore I creep into the kitchen and make myself a cup of coffee. I don't think I have woken my mother. I am wrong.

"Is my night bird already up?" I hear her voice.

"How could you possibly hear me, Mom? I was hardly breathing."

"I know you. You have always been an early riser. I never needed to drag you out of bed to go to school. Other mothers had dramas with their children every morning. I didn't even need to wake you."

"Maybe because it was Dad who woke us," I say, hoping to have the last word.

"And who do you think woke him?" she replies, pursing her lips.

However much she loves us, she has never allowed us to have the last word.

I am not going to get any reading done right now. I ask if she would like a cup of coffee too.

"And what are we going to do at this early hour? Go to the olive groves? No, I'm going to doze for a bit longer, now my little boy is home. No doubt you want to read."

"Are you sure?"

"I'm sure."

I HAD LEFT MY father in the mountain village of Richea, happy with his wife and son—but that happiness was to be a beautiful, fleeting dream.

In January 1926 came unexpected tragedy. A sudden illness, meningitis, took my beloved wife from my arms, and our two-year-old son lost his mother. For two days she wrestled with death. It was a hard winter— three feet of snow in the village. It took seven hours for the doctor to reach us by mule from Molai, along icy, snow-covered roads. Wasted effort. He didn't get there in time. She had died. The whole village mourned her. Everyone came to her funeral, in spite of the deep snow. She was buried in the churchyard in Richea, and there she lies on the mountainside directly opposite the village. A marble cross marks the spot where she sleeps. May her memory endure for all eternity.

I must ask the reader to forgive this abrupt break, but I just can't read on. I had visited Richea during one of my previous trips and sought out her grave. Her headstone had fallen over, and we put it back up. Twenty-two-year-old Maria from the well-off middle classes in Constantinople, who had fed my fantasies when I realized that my father had been married before, was still there. I met people who had known her and attended her funeral. She came alive for me, and I assume that was what my father meant when he wrote: "May her memory endure for all eternity."

Eternity isn't very long. It begins when the newborn child opens its eyes, and ends when the same child closes its eyes a while later.

Then an eternity has passed.

WITH A SENSE OF having touched on a grief that was too great and much too distant to fit inside my heart, I carry on reading.

I unexpectedly found myself in a tragic situation. What would become of the poor child? Who would show it tenderness, whose gentle hand would provide the caresses the boy so badly needed?

I was forced to turn to my sister Chariklea in Piraeus, and ask her to come to us. She had left the Black Sea with her parents-in-law and her three children, and was living in a refugee camp. She came with her children, and her company was a great relief. And so the winter of 1926 passed.

In the summer break we traveled to Macedonia—
me and my boy, Giorgios, to look for my mother and
my other siblings, while Chariklea and her children
were on their way to see her mother-in-law, who had
left Piraeus to settle in the area around the city of
Kastoria. My sister wanted to stay there in the hope
that her husband, who had been detained by the Turks,
would return.

We parted company in Thessaloniki. Chariklea
headed for Kastoria, while Giorgios and I took the
train to Kato Poroia, searching for our family. There
I heard that my mother and my brothers Panagiotis
and Giannis, along with my widowed sister Elisavet
and her two children Elias and Sofia had left Turkey in
1922. They were among the huge number of refugees
from Trebizond who had gathered in the harbor and
lived in inhumane conditions on the shore for several
days and nights. Many died there, until a ship from
the International Red Cross picked up all those who
had been lucky enough to survive and took them to
Thessaloniki.

From there some made their way to the agricultural
regions of Macedonia, while others remained in the city.

My mother and my siblings made their home in a
half-ruined Bulgarian village by the name of Lozista,
which was later changed to Mesolofs. The Greek state
allocated a plot of land and seeds to each family, along
with a house to live in.

Our family consisted of three separate families.
My mother and her youngest son, Giannis; my brother

Panagiotis and his wife; and my sister Elisavet and her children. In that way those who had survived the bestiality of the Turks and the trials of life as refugees were gathered in the same village.

And that was where I found my mother and my siblings in August 1926, after a separation of fourteen years.

Our reunion was very moving.

My mother embraced her son and grandson. She wept inconsolably, and almost drowned her motherless grandchild in tears.

I was so happy to see my mother and my siblings again. Everyone was happy. They had managed to survive countless terrible ordeals. They had found humanity and support. Once again they owned fields and a home. They were standing on Greek soil. They were not living from morning until night with the fear of slavery under the Turks. It was over. Never again would they hear the dreadful *kiopek giaour*—"faithless dog."

Their village was beautiful, with lots of running water, and the land was fertile. In addition, many of the other inhabitants were refugees from the same village by the Black Sea—a few were even relatives.

The days passed quickly, and it was time for me to return to Richea and my duties.

At the beginning of September I took my leave of my mother and my siblings. Sadly, that was the last time I kissed my mother's hand. She passed away in the winter of 1929 at the age of sixty, following a severe cold.

It was impossible for me to attend her funeral. My siblings escorted her to her final rest.

My beloved mother was illiterate, like most women in those days. However, she was energetic and intelligent, and she loved education. She had a good heart, never lost courage, and always did what she could for her children. Calm and peaceful, she had the best relationship with all her neighbors. Before she passed she managed to get Giannis to marry a girl called Andronike, who was also a refugee. She was the one who took care of my mother when she fell ill, and she was the one who was by her side during her final hours. My brother Giannis had a boy and two girls. He was quick-witted and inventive. He turned his hand to many different things, earned a lot of money without acquiring anything permanent. He was a spendthrift and a friend of nightlife, as well as a gambler. He died very young in 1942, leaving his wife a widow and her three children fatherless.

I worked alone in the school in Richea for another year. In September 1929 a second teacher was appointed, which was a relief.

My biggest worry was that I also had to take care of my son, who was growing with each day and needed me more and more. How could I leave a three-year-old boy alone? Most days I took him with me to school, where he sat at a desk along with the other children. He was calm, didn't talk, didn't fight, just listened attentively to the teacher.

However, this couldn't go on forever. I decided to embark on a second marriage.

On December 27, 1927, I married Antonia, the daughter of Stylianos Kyriazakos, from Molai. We spent our honeymoon in Richea. On a freezing cold but sunny morning in January 1928, we and the bride's dowry were collected by four bearers.

At sunset we stood on the top of Koulohéra, the mountain above the village—its name means "The One-Armed." The people of Richea came to bid us welcome with fiddles and flutes, and to see the bride, who really was beautiful.

And so a long bridal procession formed. The musicians were at the forefront, with fiddles and wind instruments, then came the newlyweds riding on mules, which were adorned for the occasion with multicolored handwoven blankets. Finally the people, laughing and joking. After an hour we reached the steep track leading down to our home.

Another surprise. The wedding feast was ready—generously prepared and laid out by the best housewives in the village. Everyone gathered in the main room. The party and the dancing went on until long after midnight. All the men got to dance with the bride and all the women with the bridegroom, according to the local custom.

That was how I built up my family once more.

My child, who had lost a mother's love at such an early age, found it again with my new wife. Not only that, my mother-in-law Maria became a genuine grandmother and my father-in-law a true grandfather.

That was how my mother had entered my father's life, which she had shared for almost fifty-five years. But the information was sparse. How had it come about? My mother was born in 1914, my father in 1890, so at the time of the wedding he was thirty-eight and she was fourteen. I really did want to know how it had come about. This was going to require a balcony conversation.

I had set myself the task of finishing the text, but I'm not too reliable on promises made to myself. I close the notebook and get up.

A while later my mother gets up too, and immediately realizes that something is wrong.

"I can see from your face that you have something on your mind," she says.

I want a gentle start, so I suggest we should have coffee on the balcony. It is a glorious morning, the exhaust fumes have not yet conquered the sky, you can see the surrounding mountains in the blue haze, and for once the dog opposite is quiet.

My mother is pleased. She has news for me.

"I remembered what day I was born. It was a Saturday, in the evening."

"Did you just remember that now?"

She sighs. "Nobody had ever asked me before."

"Do you remember what day you got married?"

"Oh yes—like it was yesterday."

She has already worked out where I am going, and intends to make me pay dearly. That is why her answers are so short.

Best to put my cards on the table.

"How come you got married so young?"

She looks at me in her characteristic way, with twinkling eyes and pursed lips, although there is a certain hesitation in her expression, as if she isn't sure it's a good idea to talk about this.

"It's such a long time ago," she says eventually.

My imagination doesn't let me down. I immediately picture the fourteen-year-old girl being dragged to the altar, not to mention my thoughts about the wedding night. At the same time, I begin to have my doubts. Do I have the right to ask these questions?

"You don't need to tell me if you don't want to," I say in a tone that carries both insinuation and sympathy.

"It was simpler than it looks."

My mother has decided to talk.

Apparently my maternal grandfather, who didn't have regular work at the time, happened to be in Richea with another man, a professional stonemason, carrying out some minor repairs at the school. There he got to know the teacher, a widower with a three-year-old boy in his arms. My grandfather liked small children and got along easily with them. Instead of concentrating on the repairs, he played with the child. My grandmother also became curious about the widowed teacher. On the pretext of visiting her husband she traveled to Richea and was captivated by the widower and his son, who immediately took to her and started calling her "Grandma." The next step was easy. She had a daughter at home, who according to the traditions back then was nearly—but not quite—old enough to marry. The girl also had a fine figure and was mature for her age.

One evening after supper she tentatively asked her daughter how she would react if someone proposed to her. The girl was horrified. "Are you tired of me?" she asked her parents, but she agreed to take a look at the widower, who in turn had been worked on by the mayor of Richea himself. "She's a young, strong girl from a decent family— you know them. There's no money, and no chattels either. But you must admit there aren't many young women lining up outside your door. Who wants a widower with a small child?"

Facts are facts. My father had never ignored them. And so an initial meeting was arranged, although it wasn't a real meeting, between the potential couple.

It was a Sunday afternoon. My father was to sit outside the café in Molai, and his potential bride would walk past, accompanied by her mother. No doubt he had shaved twice that day, trimmed his mustache, polished his shoes, ironed his shirt and pants. Was he also wearing a flower in his lapel?

My mother hadn't noticed. She saw a skinny man with wavy hair and blue-gray eyes sitting there with his legs crossed.

He saw a fully grown young woman in a long skirt, a head taller than her mother. My mother had put on stock-ings for the first time in her life—they were a present from her grandmother. The brand was Caprice. They were beige. Her well-shaped legs certainly did them justice. My father had been told she had just turned eighteen, although she looked younger.

"That's right, they tricked him," my mother says.

"But what did you think of him at the time?"

"He looked nice. And he was. He was a real man. I was given all the time I needed, and I gradually learned to respect him, to like him, and to love him. Although in the beginning the little boy was the most important thing. We got along right away. He wanted to know whose daughter I was. 'I'm your new mommy,' I said. He thought I'd come to play with him, which was exactly what I did. Running a home wasn't difficult. My mother had taught me, and your father never complained about anything. He praised my cooking to the skies. 'Food from your hands is a joy, Antonia, even if it's a month old,' he said. That meant a lot to me. I know that kind of thing doesn't count nowadays, but back then it was different. He was a teacher, he had read a great deal, but he never looked down on me. 'I wish I had your mind,' he would say. Suddenly I was the teacher's wife. People looked up to me. I was fourteen years old, but everyone listened to me. I had my own home and a wonderful little boy. That wasn't a bad situation. I really loved your brother from the first moment, as if I had given birth to him myself."

She pauses briefly, then looks at me and smiles.

"Happy now?"

Not exactly. I would have preferred a major drama about a little barefoot suitor lurking in the bushes, who was so upset that he left the village, went to America, became as rich as Croesus, and never stopped loving my mother. I just have to accept that life is not a novel.

I am just about to say so when the phone rings.

"I expect that's your brother."

It is my brother, informing us that he has booked a table at a restaurant where he knows the owner, and that he will pick us up outside the apartment building at precisely seven o'clock.

"*Jawohl, mein Führer.*"

"Go fuck yourself."

We end the call.

LOVE IS LIKE ROME. With a bit of luck, all roads lead there. My mother goes into the kitchen and fetches a box of fresh beans, which she cleans with the skill of at least eighty years. You have to strip off the long fibers at the sides, but without—and this is where the problems start—breaking up the beans, which is easily done.

Her ninety-two-year-old hands, marked with age spots, seem to work of their own volition. She doesn't even look at what she is doing. She hasn't removed her smooth wedding ring for more than seventy-eight years and the skin has grown around it, as sometimes happens with the trunks of old oak trees. They grow around a foreign object, embrace it, make it their own.

Is that perhaps the goal of love?

I don't know, just as I don't really know what love is. In Seattle a long time ago, I once got into conversation with a renowned neurophysiologist, who was unhappily in love and explained to me that love didn't actually serve any purpose, nor did the pleasure of orgasm. Nature didn't need to compensate us in order to make us procreate; we would do it anyway. From this he drew the conclusion that love was a human invention and an unnecessary one, but oh so real.

As I sit there next to my mother watching her prepare the beans, I amuse myself by making a quick list of the ways in which we fall in love. Here it is:

1. Love at first sight.
   You see someone, and that's it. This happens frequently both in life and in literature. It is impossible to know what is aroused within us. They say it is a chemical union, recognizing yourself in the other person, having the sense that you have been waiting for him or her all your life, and so on. Basically the whole thing is inexplicable, but extremely tangible. I once knew a man who saw a woman walking down a flight of stairs. That was enough. He never forgot her. It is generally accepted that this instant infatuation usually comes to an end within three to six months, but in the case I mentioned, it lasted a lifetime.

2. The slow acclimatization.
   You meet someone you have to live with, for various reasons. You don't have any strong feelings, you take one day at a time, and slowly comes the realization that you have started to like the person in question. That

was what happened to my parents, like many millions of others on this earth. The advantage of falling in love in this way is that it leads to a long life together, while those who experience the instant kind can only hope for this outcome. In other words, the slow love proceeds from what the instant love wants to achieve.

3. Falling in love through hearsay.
You have never met the other person, but you have heard about them. Even the ancient Greeks were aware of this variant. Paris, the prince of Troy, had never met Helen of Sparta, but he knew that she was regarded as the most beautiful woman in the world. He was in love in advance, and there could only be one outcome. He ran away with her, she left her husband, and the very first world war had begun.

4. Falling in love through words.
The classic example here is Cyrano de Bergerac. The poor man had a nose like mine, and didn't dare show himself to his love. He therefore asked another young man to woo her, while he stood in the background whispering. The girl sees the young man but hears Cyrano's words, and even though the young man is beautiful, the words are more beautiful. Guess who wins her in the end?

5. Falling in love because of the way the other person feels.
You meet someone you don't really care about, but this person falls in love with you, at which point you fall in

love out of sheer curiosity about what he or she sees in you. Very common in nineteenth-century novels.

6. Falling in love through illusion.
   You don't care about the person in question, but you do care about some particular quality, power or wealth or reputation, which you would like to share, and eventually you become "suitably" in love. This type is widely represented in so-called developmental novels.

7. Falling in love through revenge.
   You don't care about the person in question, but you want to prevent someone else from having them. Often occurs in large families, and between friends.

8. Falling in love through falling in love.
   There are quite simply people who have to be in love if life is to be worth living. They are constantly newly smitten, their choices are extremely varied, there is room in their heart for just about everything.

9. Falling in love for ideological reasons.
   Very common in closed circles of all kinds. If the leader says that you must love someone, then you make sure you do, not to please the person in question or yourself but the leader.

10. Falling in love through lies.
    You have falsely claimed to be in love with someone for such a long time that eventually you believe it yourself.

Younger men are especially susceptible to this variant, as they are not mature enough to distinguish between the gates of heaven and the fires of hell.

11. Falling in love à la Plato.
You insist that you are in love not in a physical sense but only spiritually. Why you then end up in bed is a mystery, but that is exactly what happens.

12. Love in general.
This category covers all the types I haven't thought of, but I'm convinced they exist.

I close my notebook.

While I have been making my list, my mother has prepared two pounds of beans, and now wants to know what my father had written about her.

"He said you were a real mother to Giorgios, and a beautiful bride."

She likes that. For a brief moment she sits completely still, then she runs a hand over her gray hair, lightly and slowly as only a fourteen-year-old girl can do.

Then she says, "You boys couldn't have had a better father. And I couldn't have had a better husband. A wonderful human being. And a real man, right to the end!"

Have I heard her correctly? Does she really want to be so open? I decide to seize the opportunity.

"Yes, but he was nearly twenty-five years older than you. Were you never tempted by a younger man?"

There is a deathly silence, and I wish I'd kept my mouth shut.

"We didn't do that kind of thing in my day. We didn't spread our legs. The very thought of it would have made me die of shame. I realize times have changed, I can see that on TV and with all these divorces. It was different back then. Women became widowed in their thirties and dressed in black for the rest of their lives. I don't know if that was better. Maybe not. But there is only one way to live: The way you can live your life. The shame was real to us—more real than most things."

I was a child of a different time. Why should you be ashamed of lusting after someone other than your legal spouse? I didn't think that was necessary. I felt shame in relation to professional failures, or when I had made a fool of myself. To me, shame was an emotion like any other. To my mother it was a key aspect of her life.

Lately I have noticed that a new category of people has appeared: They don't even know what shame is. Worse, they are proud of not knowing. Conscience seems to be following the fashion in bikinis—the smaller the better.

My mother is right about one thing—you can only live the life you are capable of living.

It looks like a truism, but it isn't. Most unhappiness comes from trying to live lives that we are not capable of living.

"I'm going in," my mother says.

It is time to start thinking about lunch, which will be simple fare as we are going out in the evening.

She serves fresh beans in tomato sauce with feta, a couple of grilled homemade burgers with lots of oregano, thyme, and lemon. We drink chilled retsina and toast each other and all those who aren't here—a long list.

On this occasion I am actually allowed to do the dishes, because my mother has a slight pain in her back—this happens at regular intervals.

> *But it is nothing.*
> *I take my medicine,*
> *A Bayer aspirin*
> *And I am fine,*

she declaims as she retires to her room.

"You'll live to be a hundred, Mom," I call after her.

"Why only a hundred, if you please? Promise to visit me now and again and I don't think I'll ever die."

THE SPOT WHERE I have my sofa bed is cool. From the apartments all around come the usual sounds of eating, talking, washing dishes. Gradually it all dies away, stopping completely at about three o'clock as people settle down to rest. The younger couples make love. The children sleep, or pretend to.

My mother finds it difficult to get to sleep and wakes easily. She learned to do this when she had a child. The constant anxiety, especially during the war, although the worst time was after the war when Greek was fighting Greek. Where are the children? What are the children doing? Have you seen the children? If you couldn't see the children, you were beside yourself with worry. That worry has never really left her. It will never leave her.

My father liked to rest in the middle of the day, even if it was only for ten minutes. He also had a theory to support this preference. "Have you ever seen an animal running around after it's eaten?" he would say. The direct opposite of Leonardo da Vinci, who claimed that the key to good health was a walk after lunch. Then again he didn't live to be as old as my father, whose ability both to fall asleep and to wake instantly was astonishing. He had probably learned it in the army, but also in other places, as we shall soon see.

I open his narrative again. How could he maintain such clear, beautiful handwriting in old age? Not once do I have to look more closely at the text, long passages set out in symmetrical lines.

I served at the school in Richea for eight years. I came to love these people very much, and worked for their progress. I didn't content myself with my main duties but also tried to help them improve both culturally and financially. Together with Dr. Theodor Stavropolous and other forward-thinking individuals, we formed a society for the replanting of forests in Koulohéra, for the cultivation of orchards, enabling the grafting of thousands of crab apple and wild olive trees. We started a monthly local newspaper and a reading room with a library, where the young people of the village gathered on Sundays. A group of them gave theater performances.

In Koulohéra there is to this day an area of pine trees known as "Kallifatides' forest." For my social work outside the school the Education Department awarded me a diploma of honor and a thousand drachma on September 26, 1934, see government newsletter number 92.

In September 1932 I was transferred to the school in Molai, where I had many excellent colleagues. Unfortunately the school itself was cramped and dilapidated. However, with the help of the local residents and the state, we soon had a two-story building.

Our life in Molai was pleasant, and my work at the school even more pleasant.

Molai is the largest settlement in the province, and the location for all the state and municipal authorities: courthouses, banks, the tax office, the high school. The market supplied everything you could possibly need. We were also close to my wife's parents, not strangers among strangers.

On December 27, 1932, in my second marriage I had another boy, christened Stelios after my father-in-law. On March 13, 1938, our last child, Theodor, was born.

This is a surprise. On my passport and all my other documents it states that I was born on the twelfth, not the thirteenth. Presumably someone, probably my grandmother, thought that the thirteenth was not a favorable date on which to come into the world.

On the other hand, what does it really matter? There may be some uncertainty about which day I was born, but none about the fact that I was. You don't have to be Descartes to establish that you exist, if nothing else as a hindrance to others. So I continue reading.

And so our family was complete, and our life together was full of enjoyment and hope. Giorgios was at the high school and Stelios the elementary school when the Second World War, which shook us all to the core, suddenly began on October 28, 1940.

On April 1, 1941, our country was occupied by Germans and Italians. I am leaving out the global events, which are well known, and limiting myself to those elements that affect me and my family. The years of the occupation are burned into my memory forever. Misery and starvation everywhere. Everything edible went to the occupying forces. Stores closed, and desperate parents couldn't find anything to buy for their children, who grew thinner and thinner until they resembled living skeletons. Gangs of emaciated children searching through the garbage in the hope of finding a bone to lick were a common sight.

In the towns and cities, the situation was unbearable. In the country we could just about get by. The blessed earth always provides something to chew on. For that reason, people moved up into the mountains. Some sought out their relatives. My family wasn't as short of food as others during this difficult time, largely because the schools were closed, and many farmers sent their children to us for private lessons so that they wouldn't forget what they had learned. They paid us in kind—a little olive oil, cheese, bread, other things they could do without.

But it wasn't only the hunger. The occupying forces managed to spread the poison of discord among us. Some cooperated with them, others fought against them. Many left their homes and formed partisan units, which struck wherever they could gain access to the enemy and cause transport problems for them.

The occupiers retaliated by burning down buildings and killing whoever happened to be in their way, including war invalids. Betrayal and informing on individuals. Concentration camps in the big cities. The smallest accusation was enough for a person to end up in jail. Eventually I too fell victim.

One evening in June 1944 the Germans arrested me in the yard of our home in Molai and locked me inside a house. They bound my arms and legs and left me lying on the floor. All night the German soldiers ate and drank, they sang and got drunk.

In the morning they untied me and took me with them on foot to Sparta, where they threw me in jail.

Once again my father left out many details. Fortunately I had access to the true archive: my mother.

According to her, it was the photograph of him from the First World War in his Turkish lieutenant's uniform with the Turkish War Medal and the German Iron Cross on his breast that saved his life on that occasion. When the

Germans searched the house, they saw it on the sideboard in the dining room. *"Aber er ist ein Held!"* the German captain had said. My mother didn't understand; the captain had repeated it several times, so she learned the sentence by heart and her father translated it for her some time later. *But he is a hero!*

Here we have an example of the dramatic completion of pure chance. Chekhov always said that if you hang a pistol on the wall in Act One, then it has to be fired in Act Three. What applied to a theatrical drama also seemed to apply to life. A photograph of a young man who has just saved several lives then saves his own life twenty years later.

My grandmother had a different way of saying the same thing. "Do a good deed and throw it in the sea," she would urge us—meaning that it would always come back to us.

I also had a memory from that time which the great archivist—my mother—insists cannot be true. I was convinced that I took some food to my father in his temporary prison. I could see him lying on the floor, in the cellar of a café that also served as a newsstand and bookstore. My mother insists that neither she nor anyone else would think of sending me—a six-year-old boy—to take food to my father. But how come I remember it so clearly? Have I dreamed it?

They can say what they like. I have no intention of trying to forget what I remember. My father didn't do that either.

The following morning they took me to the Gestapo for interrogation. It was the usual accusation: I was a

Communist. They treated me with extreme violence.
They whipped me with barbed wire, then took me back
to jail with blood pouring down all over my body. After
a week they brought me in for another interrogation.

The torture was repeated. This time they subjected
my wounded body to all the tools their evil fantasy
could come up with. Electric shocks, mock executions
with random shots. I was unconscious when they took
me back to my cell.

I am surprised to find myself sobbing helplessly. I am
afraid that my mother will hear me.

How could he ever smile again after that? How could he
carry on loving, caring about life?

I would really like to know what they asked him about,
what they wanted him to say that he refused to reveal.

There must have been an interpreter.

Who had informed on him, and why?

Was my father secretly a member of the resistance,
or was it just blind evil that persecuted him, like so many
others?

I would like to know.

I get up from the sofa and rinse my face in cold water.
Needless to say I manage to wake my mother.

"Would you like a 'youthful' cup of coffee?" she asks
immediately.

The term is a joke between us, referring to a fresh cup
of coffee, and I no longer remember how it came about.

I say yes, and soon we are sitting opposite each other
on the balcony once more. All around us the city is coming

back to life. I feel calmer inside. On the balconies opposite us, people begin to water their plants.

"How did he cope with what happened to him in jail, Mom?"

I can almost see the darkness fall over her eyes.

"I don't know. The skinny refugee from the Black Sea, who had already lost everything. I asked him the same question. 'Antonia,' he said, 'it was the child, our young-est, that I pictured before me the whole time. What would become of him if something happened to me?'"

I am about to cry again. I see that she has tears in her eyes. I have to do something. We are not going to spend this serene afternoon in tears. Sometimes you just have to get a grip on yourself. That was what my father had done. Once, a long time ago, I had asked him what it felt like to stand in front of the firing squad, to hear the shot and not know whether you are dead or alive. "I came up with an idea," he had replied. "I stood on one leg, like a stork. If the leg gave way, then I would know that I was dead."

"How is your back, Mom?"

"Now I see you, it doesn't hurt at all."

It's just a matter of seeing each other. Of fighting the old fear of losing sight of each other.

"I'll never forget when he came back from jail. He brought the supplies the Red Cross had given him for the journey. He hadn't even opened the packet. He'd saved it for you. 'Antonia, this is for the children,' he said. God for-give me, but He doesn't make people like that any more. Nowadays these dogs and bitches leave their children so they can fuck each other!"

"Mom!"

"Sometimes you have to tell it like it is. Are these men fathers? Are these women mothers? No!"

She continues for some time in the same vein, until I realize what she is doing. She is playing a part in order to chase away my sorrow. Once I understand I join in, and we have great fun with our noble competition to badmouth today's men and women as much as we can, while all along knowing we are wrong. The world always produces heroes and heroines, unfortunately. We see the sacrifices that the Albanians and other refugees make for their children all around us, every single day.

We sit there until my mother decides it is time to start getting ready for the evening.

"But we've got plenty of time," I object.

"I want to be ready. I know your brother, I know what a dictator he is! If we're not down there dead on time he'll play merry hell."

This is true. It is also true that I would want to do the same, under certain circumstances. It isn't easy to forget what you remember, but sometimes you have to try.

There is one question my mother has always liked to ask.

"What do you think I should wear?"

I think for a moment. I really want her to wear the floral dress she had on when we walked to the market, with my hand safely in hers, sixty years ago.

"The black skirt with a white blouse and your cardigan, in case it gets chilly later."

"Won't I look old, wearing a cardigan? I might as well take my walking stick, like my grandmother."

In the end she opts for the black skirt with a dark green blouse and no stick. She also puts on a pearl necklace and the ring my brother gave her for her ninetieth birthday.

And so the question she liked to ask is resolved.

Next comes the question she likes to be asked.

"Shall I put on my suit?"

She doesn't even bother to look at me.

"No. I think you should put on your track suit and sneakers. Of course you need to wear your suit! I've ironed your white shirt, and you've forgotten to bring a tie, but it'll have to do... At least your neck isn't hanging down like a goose's neck. Not yet."

And so that question is also resolved.

The evening has gotten off to a promising start.

THE RESTAURANT IS SITUATED high on one of the hills. When I was a little boy they were known as Turkovoúnia, the Turkish Mountains. I have no idea what they are called now. There isn't much left of them; the new-build nation has eaten its way right up to the top.

"Is this okay?" my brother asks.

"I could sit here all night," my mother replies.

The view from the dining room is fantastic, but the immediate environment is more problematic.

"Do you think they could turn the music down?" I ask.

"Why not?" As I said earlier, my brother knows the owner. "We can ask them to turn it off completely."

"We don't need to behave like the fly," my mother remarks.

We look at her—my sister-in-law, my brother, me, and their son, who asks, "What do you mean, Grandma?"

She smiles. "Haven't you heard the saying?"

"What saying?"

"Since the fly got an ass, she shits on all of us."

I don't really get the point, but the image of a fly with a huge ass is certainly innovative. My nephew wants a more detailed explanation.

"We mustn't go over the top. Going over the top is always bad. There's another saying, if you would like to improve your education before we eat."

We would.

"We told the old woman she was allowed to fart, but not all the time."

"Lovely. If it's not shit, it's farting, just as we're about to eat." My brother moans.

At that moment the waiter arrives to take our order. There is some confusion until my brother takes over and orders for everyone. In less than five minutes an array of small plates appears on our table with all kinds of appetizing dishes: tzatziki, eggplant salad, caviar with crème fraîche, little cheese quiches, olives, feta, fried potatoes. The main course is grilled kid, which tastes divine. Naturally we drink retsina, about which an English wine expert once wrote: "It is considered by the Greeks as wine."

The conversation starts off as a collective discussion but gradually becomes fragmented, which is slightly tricky as eventually we don't really know who we are talking to, let alone who is talking to us. Questions and answers fly back and forth across the table in all directions, and in the middle of the tumult I pick up the term "coup d'état."

It has come from my brother, and I ask what he is referring to.

"This was the route the tanks took on the night of April 21, 1967. Do you remember, Mom?"

"How could I forget? The entire building shook. I thought it was an earthquake. 'It's not an earthquake,' said your late father. 'It's the Fascists coming back.' He was deathly pale. But we didn't do too badly…except that the secret police came and warned us against keeping in contact with you. 'He denigrates our country,' they said, 'and those blue-eyed Swedes listen to him.'"

That was me. I remember how difficult I found it to process what had happened back home in Greece. I was living in student housing in Solna when another Greek student came and knocked on my door. He had heard about the coup on the morning news on the radio.

I didn't understand. Was it possible to seize power just like that?

Apparently so. Three colonels and some tanks took a stranglehold on the entire country. The whole thing was over in a few hours, and they remained in power for several years.

"They threatened me too," my brother says. "Tell your little brother to keep his thoughts to himself, otherwise…"

The circle was closed. First the children pay for their father's political actions. Then the fathers pay for the children's actions. The sin that stretches both forward and backward. Intransigence is the real original sin.

"Those were difficult years," my mother says. "When you walked past the building where the secret police operated, you could hear people screaming as they were tortured. God knows we've had a great deal to bear. But now the colonels are gone, while we are still here."

This is the signal to change the subject, which we do, although I don't manage to shake it off completely. The shame I had felt at that time was too great. I was in Sweden, living a fairly pleasant student life, while my family, my ex-girlfriends, my old friends lived in fear. Some of them languished in jail, and one young woman lost her child in there as a result of all the abuse she suffered.

This shame sometimes found its expression in pathetic ways. I once got up in the middle of the night and tore my sheets to shreds, because their whiteness symbolized the blank face of treachery. I even swore a sacred oath that I would not sleep with anyone until Greece was free again. I don't need to go into how that went. Let's just say I didn't become a hero of the freedom movement.

Anyway, we have a successful evening, which my mother brings to a close with the ritual phrase: "We ate well on this day too. Bravo, Stelios!"

He is praised for having chosen the right restaurant. I, who have paid for everything, get nothing.

There is, as I said, some justice in everything.

Like another saying: Some fuck and others pay.

I refrain from saying it, but that doesn't mean I'm not thinking it. How come there are so many sayings in Greek? There is hardly a situation that isn't covered. Vanity, shamelessness, hubris, greed, lust. The Greeks have quite simply been there before, to the extent that they have had time to formulate an appropriate comment.

Every saying is a narrative in the most naked, totally elementary form. Some reach us from long, long ago. It might be an utterance from poets like Homer, or wise men like the lawgiver Solon of Athens, almost six hundred years BC, or Lycurgus of Sparta. They might be the view of elderly philosophers, which later became misunderstood or paraphrased. These ancient narratives live on in our language, and above all they live on in our lives as standards and templates for how a life should be lived.

They even exist as jokes. Amalias, a small town in Greece, was famous in ancient times for its watermelons, and for its inhabitants' intellectual similarity with those watermelons. It is still famous for the same things.

I am trying to prove not the homogeneity of Greek culture but the superior power of narrative. It lives on, even if everything else all around has changed. It lives with us, and we live within it. It is the rushing torrent that carries life along with it.

First came the myth, said the ancient Greeks, and then came reason.

I fear a world without reason as much as a world with only reason.

And so the fifth day with my mother is over. High above the city we can enjoy all the light below us, which is getting closer and closer as we drive down the hill.

Is there anything more wonderful than approaching the light?

It is almost like being reborn.

THE SIXTH DAY

I HAVE A FEW pages left of my father's text, and I want to finish it while I am still in Athens and able to complement it with my mother's testimony.

We get up quite late and have breakfast in silence. My mother looks composed. I think it is because my departure is getting closer.

I am wrong. She has a major undertaking before her on this day. She is going to bake a certain kind of cookie called kourambiedes, which according to her have earned her immortal renown.

"Anyone who has tasted my kourambiedes has never forgotten them," she says.

This is a constant bone of contention between us. Not that I doubt her skill, but I have no desire to fill my suitcase with cookies that she wants me to take back to Sweden, to my wife, to my father-in-law, to my daughter-in-law, to my children and grandchildren.

"To think you've become a grandfather!"

I concede that it is a miracle, but it doesn't mean she has to bake kourambiedes, I can buy a tin at the airport. Which is true. Kourambiedes are an export product.

"Maybe you can, but I want your family to taste mine. There's not much else I can do for them. They're not here!"

(And there it is: the bitter complaint that I have robbed her not only of my presence but that of my family. As the saying has it: My child's child is twice my child.)

"You don't need to do anything for them. They have plenty of everything."

"Not my kourambiedes!"

I realize that she has made up her mind, and there isn't much I can do about it. I also hate myself for being so petty and trying to stop her from being the person she is: a woman who always thinks about everyone else.

Why do I do it? Simply because I can't handle certain situations. For example, what if Swedish customs check my suitcase at Arlanda Airport? What could be more embarrassing than them finding small homemade cookies in there? In my suitcase? As if I couldn't afford to buy them. It would be like taking your own packed lunch to a restaurant, openly advertising your poverty. Showing that you can't afford something.

There is a shame in poverty that most people have forgotten. Which is good. But I haven't managed to do that. Which is also good, except when it goes too far. During all my years in Sweden I have come into contact with the welfare authorities only once.

It was Christmas. I didn't have a single krona in my

pocket. Not one. I was given a hundred kronor by social services in Solna. I almost died of shame. It was stupid. We shouldn't have to feel like that. But there we find ourselves in the same situation as when we have to forget what we remember.

How can I feel differently, when I feel the way I feel?

My wife has never had any problem at all with a batch of kourambiedes. She happily accepts everything my Greek family gives her. Cookies, olives, feta. When we arrive at Arlanda I hang back, not wishing to be associated with the woman who is smuggling food into Sweden.

That's just the way it is, unfortunately.

The difference is clear. She accepts a gift as proof of love and care, while I regard it as charity.

The difference can be made even clearer.

She was born in the rich part of the world.

I was born in the poor part.

This is why, among other reasons, wealthy countries cannot always help their poorer counterparts. When the rich give, it is charity. When the poor give, it is solidarity. Charity helps the rich to assuage their conscience, but it changes nothing. Solidarity, on the other hand, can change the world.

Consequently, poor countries can help one another more than wealthy countries can help them.

I realize that I am turning a few cookies into a global problem and decide to leave my mother in peace and return to my own task, which will however require a cup of "youthful" coffee.

"Go and sit on the balcony, I'll bring it out to you," my mother says, and we are friends again.

She comes and sits down too.

"What about the kourambiedes?" I ask.

"I've got all day. Right now I want to sit here with my boy, who will soon be leaving."

There is no obvious sorrow in her words. Her tone is almost conspiratorial, indicating a mutual understanding between us.

"I know you miss your family."

I settle for shaking my head.

It is another Athenian morning. Open sky, sunshine, street traders, barking dogs, screaming children. And yet such calmness within my soul, such peace of mind.

"Your brother was in fine form yesterday. If you only knew how proud of you he is. Even when he was little he was proud. He was six years old when you were born, and do you know what he said? 'Now I've got another brother, I'd like to see the person who would dare to fight with me!'"

"Speaking of which—Dad writes that I was born on March thirteenth. I've always believed it was the twelfth. So which is correct?"

My mother thinks for a moment.

"It was the night between the twelfth and the thirteenth. So we went for the twelfth."

"In other words, my life began with a lie!" I say theatrically.

"To tell the truth, I don't really remember. In those days we didn't look at the clock very often. We didn't wear watches. In fact, we didn't have any clocks. The mayor had a clock. The judge, the pharmacist, your late father. It was morning, the middle of the day, afternoon, or evening. No one said, 'It's a quarter to three.' Who cared about a quarter of an hour? No olives or grapes ripen in a quarter of an hour. I got my first watch at the age of forty. It was a Venus. It's still around somewhere. Your late father explained to me that Venus was a goddess, but I've forgotten what kind of goddess she was."

"The goddess of beauty."

"Oh yes, that's right. But as for your birthday, I do remember the dinner your grandfather organized to celebrate."

She starts to laugh. I know I have a few trying minutes ahead. As I said earlier, my mother is incapable of telling a funny story. She laughs more than anyone else, and she doesn't always reach the end because she is already writhing in paroxysms of laughter.

"So tell me about this dinner," I say impatiently.

"He'd bought an enormous fish, which he carried home in a bucket of water to keep it fresh…" (she is laughing so much that it takes a huge effort for her to continue) "…but the blessed fish wasn't just fresh, it was still alive, and when he took it out…" (she definitely can't carry on now, she is almost hysterical, her eyes fill with tears and she rubs them with her knuckles, like a child, while I wait for the punch line) "…he dropped it on the floor and then started chasing it around with an ax…look at the bastard…it's grown feet!"

Finally she can give herself over to the entertaining memory.

"It's grown feet," she repeats several times, almost passing out with the hilarity of it all. I look at her as she tries to regain control, and I am drawn into her laughter. After a minute or so she manages to pull herself together.

"God be with you my child, you make me laugh so much."

"*I* make you laugh?"

"I'm happy now. My kourambiedes will be splendid," she says, tripping off to the kitchen with light footsteps.

I had intended to continue translating my father's text, but I decide I want to see how she makes her famous kourambiedes, so I follow her. Besides, like everything else in the strongly person-centered Greek world, kourambiedes is a suspect cookie: The word is also used to describe what is usually known as *ett mähä* in Swedish—a sop. Admittedly it is difficult to miss the difference between a person and a cookie, but not always. A friend of mine in Sweden called his wife's lover a lenten bun.

FIRST OF ALL MY mother boils a handful of almonds, which she then roasts in the oven so that she can peel them. Next she chops the white kernels into tiny pieces. She melts a pound of butter, adds a heaped teacup of sugar and stirs the mixture well. Next comes a coffee cup of Cognac, and finally the chopped almonds. She folds in two pounds of flour and kneads the mixture ferociously. This seems to be some kind of muscle memory, working independently of her body. A ninety-two-year-old woman doesn't possess that level of strength. She shapes the individual cookies and places them on a baking tray, then they go into the oven for half an hour at 175 degrees.

She takes out the tray and rolls the cookies in powdered sugar, arranges them in a plastic container, and dusts a little more powdered sugar over them.

The whole thing has taken her less than an hour and a half.

The entire apartment smells wonderful.

I RETURN TO MY father's text.

After the interrogations I was taken back to death row, where prisoners were guarded very closely. We were allowed out only twice a day, morning and evening, to do what we needed to do. We were condemned to death, awaiting execution.

During the time I spent in the jail in Sparta, the door of our cell opened only once, at midnight. A German subaltern and a Greek sergeant walked in. That night there were thirteen of us in the cell. We looked at one another, deathly pale. Whose turn was it now?

They took eleven men with them. We never saw them again. There were two of us left, me and Elias from the village of Velliés. We had no idea what was going on. It could be that those eleven filled the required quota. "We survived this time," I said. After a while we heard shots. Eleven more Greeks killed. More mothers and sisters would weep. And all this for our country.

A few days later we were transferred to the camp in Tripoli, which was also packed. However, the

Germans' behavior was less aggressive there. We had a little more freedom. There were many Italians in the camp, prisoners just like us. Toward the end of the war the former allies became deadly enemies. The Italians gave us news about the progress of the war. For four months we had been so closely confined that we knew nothing about what was going on out there. We learned that the Germans were losing the war. The Russians were getting close to the German border. We gained fresh courage.

Unfortunately the monster struck again before it gave up.

A further twenty-five Greeks from our camp were executed. The jails were thrown open on September 10, 1944. The Germans left and gathered in Athens. We were free.

How were we to get home to our families? There was no transport. We set off on foot. It took me four days from Tripoli to Molai. The good news reached Molai long before me.

I remembered it very well. We were still in the country, at my great-grandmother's farm, St. Peter, where a four-hundred-year-old chestnut tree provided cool shade from the heat of the summer. I was six years old. I stole my great-grandmother's salt and strewed it across the ground, believing that it would grow into salt trees, as my brother had told me.

Everyone except my father was there. My great-grandmother, my grandmother, my grandfather, my

brothers, my mother. On that particular afternoon I suddenly began to crawl on all fours, for no reason whatsoever.

My great-grandmother was quite taken by this.

"Are you coming or going, my child?" she asked.

"I'm coming."

She sighed with relief and called out to my mother,
"Don't be afraid, girl—your husband is coming back!"

Five minutes later, in the distance on the hot track, we
saw a black swirl of dust. It was a neighbor from the village,
Aunt Mató, running to tell us the good news.

Sixty-two years have passed since then. I no longer remember how I felt when I saw my father again, I don't remember what he said or what he was wearing.

I have forgotten how my mother and the others reacted.

But there is one thing I cannot forget: that black swirl
of dust, because Aunt Mató was dressed entirely in black.

I have seen that swirl of dust in my mind's eye in the
most unexpected situations and places.

I have seen it at Slussen in Stockholm, on the Paris
Métro, in Central Park in New York, in the French quarter
in Montreal. I see it in my dreams.

Every time my heart races.

Perhaps I am still waiting for my father.

My family was in the country, at my mother-in-law's
farm, St. Peter. They were waiting for me with great
anxiety—which was well-founded. They hadn't heard
from me in four months. After Sparta, no one knew
where we had been taken. Most people thought we

had been executed, but fate granted me the joy of surviving and returning to my family.

A year later, the whole country was free. The schools reopened and the teachers, all those who had survived, went back to their posts. Once again the schoolyards were filled with the happy sound of children playing. Our school began with a full complement of staff, as before.

Unfortunately I was thrown into jail in Sparta once again, facing the same accusation as before: Communist. The trial took place very quickly and I was released, but with the proviso that I had to remain in Sparta until further notice. And so my family lost their protector once more.

In November 1945 I was transferred to the school in the village of Magoula, not far from Sparta, and in January 1946 I was allowed to return to the school in Molai. However, I chose to go to Richea instead.

I wanted to finish my service there, close to my dear Richea residents, with whom I was united through sorrowful memories—but also many happy ones.

Sadly, my wish was not fulfilled. A number of difficult circumstances meant that I was forced to resign and travel alone to Piraeus. Antonia followed at a later date.

Here I pause. It is obvious that my father did not want to burden us by talking about what he had done for us, for example saving his provisions to give to us. Nor did he want to continue along the road of intransigence. The "difficult circumstances" of which he spoke were very concrete. My mother had already told me what had happened.

It was pure luck that he had escaped with his life. The Fascists came looking for him at home. My father happened to be in the yard and heard them. He left immediately, with only the clothes he was wearing.

"Where is your husband?" they asked my mother.

"He's gone to school," she lied, her voice trembling. She thought he was still in the yard. They accepted what she said. One of them was a relative on my grandmother's side, and he gave her a slap across the face. He probably saved her life.

My father hid until night fell, then he crept back home and said goodbye to his wife. We children were asleep. If he had stayed he would have been killed, perhaps even thrown into "the hole."

After all those years in the same province and the same villages, after having taught so many children and adults, he was and remained "the refugee from the Black Sea." A Greek who wasn't allowed to be a real Greek. Not for everyone, but for enough people.

I find it a regrettable consolation when people in Sweden talk about how difficult it is for immigrants and refugees to assimilate into society. It is difficult to get inside the walls. It has always been the same, everywhere.

Is that a reason to give up?

He didn't. In his fifty-sixth year he was once again hunted, his life hung by a fragile thread, his best friend was murdered by the Greek Fascists right in front of his children. Yet again he had to live outside the walls, just like the name of the distant area of Trebizond where he was born.

At that time my mother was thirty-two years old. He wrote only that she followed him at a later date. Nothing more.

I NEED TO KNOW everything, all the details.

On the pretext that I want to taste the freshly baked kourambiedes, I go into the kitchen, make two "youthful" coffees, and ask my mother to come and sit with me on the balcony. The sun is high in the sky, the air is warm, the dog opposite lies panting and keeps quiet.

I get straight to the point and explain what I want to know. How did she join my father in Piraeus?

And she tells me a story I have never heard before.

First of all she had to get my brother and me to our maternal grandparents. Our half brother had already gone to Athens to study at the university. He was staying with his aunt Chrisi. When we were safe, my mother set off with everything she could take from home. It wasn't much, but she did manage to transport a pig and a few hens.

That meant she had to travel by boat. She was accompanied by another woman, a dear friend who, along with her husband, had been a witness at my parents' wedding. The husband was also a wanted man, which was completely incomprehensible. He was the mayor of Richea, and one of the noblest men who had ever lived. "A saint," according to my mother, who told me that he used to go around the village with a torch in the middle of the night to see if there was anyone who needed help. During the years of starvation, he shared everything he had. "Without him many families would have gone under. But the fanatics are blind monsters," my mother says.

She and her friend reached the harbor in Gerakas, a small community deep within a long inlet, which protects it from the winds that can otherwise be violent and unpredictable there. They boarded the caïque, a small fishing boat with an engine, which was waiting for them. They left under cover of darkness, but it proved impossible for the caïque to get out onto the open sea. Mountainous waves hurtled toward them, as if they were guarding the harbor in order to prevent anyone sailing away. They had to turn back.

There was a big party at the taverna in the village, with grilled kid and lamb. People were drinking and yelling and firing shots into the air. The Fascists were celebrating the death of a resistance fighter.

That was how things were at the time.

"Everyone's greatest fear was 'the hole.' No one knew where it was, but according to the rumors it was bottomless. Anyone who was thrown into it was never found again. It was a gateway to the underworld. Dying was one thing, but never to be found again, never to have a little earth covering your body, was quite another—as if you had never existed."

The two women were terrified of being discovered, but on this occasion the darkness was on their side. They stayed the night with an acquaintance, and the following morning the wind had eased and they were able to leave. They traveled to the island of Aegina, where they were lucky enough to meet a young man who owned the restaurant in the harbor. My father had been his teacher. He invited the women in for a meal, and they continued their journey to Piraeus without any further problems. My mother still had the pig and the hens with her.

However, my father had already left Piraeus, because the Fascists were looking for him there too. He was given a roof over his head in the same place as our half brother: with Aunt Chrisi, the sister of his first wife, and her husband, Athanassios.

Life settled down, to the extent that a neighbor even stole a laying hen from my mother and locked it in her bedroom.

"'That hen ought to be regarded as a political prisoner,' your late father said. But what could I do?" my mother says with a laugh.

"What happened to the pig?"

She looks at me in her inimitable way.

"What do you think?"

Then she goes back into the kitchen to prepare lunch.

EVERY STORY EXPLAINS SOMETHING, while at the same time giving rise to fresh questions.

What had my father done to be so hated?

Perhaps he was a Communist. I don't know. A wreath appeared at his funeral: To Demetrios Kallifatides from his comrades in the resistance movement.

No one knew who had delivered the wreath, and that was the way it stayed. Had he done more than we were aware of? He had always been taciturn—was that the reason why?

Possibly, but these secrets followed him to the grave, and in any case they can't account for the fierce hatred that poisoned his remaining years.

I think there is another explanation. He wasn't one of them. He never became one of them. He never made it inside the walls. In the end they excluded him, once and for all. But he never gave up. That was his legacy to us. We never give up.

First of all my mother came to Athens. Then my brother. He traveled with a friend of the family. Thirty years later, that man's grandson is one of his students. Life goes around in circles. Eventually it was my turn to travel to Athens. I sailed in a caïque with my grandfather. On this occasion too the sea was rough, we threw up constantly, but after a long night we reached the island of Poros, where I tasted yogurt with honey in it for the first time. I have tried in vain to rediscover that flavor ever since.

Aunt Chrisi found room for us all. We were supposed to be staying for a few weeks. We remained there for several years.

In September 1947 I was forced to tender my resignation, and to request a reduced pension. I had five mouths to feed, we were guests in someone else's home, without sufficient income. I sought work in private schools. For thirteen years I worked in two private schools at the same time: in the morning from eight until two, and in the evening from six until ten. I finally took my pension in 1960, at the age of seventy. I had contributed to the education of Greek children in Turkey and in Greece for sixty-two years.

I made sure that my sons were educated.

After all those years as a teacher, I owned nothing. In 1966 I managed to buy a two-room apartment on the fourth floor in the district of Gyzi, at 41 Agiou Charalambous. It cost 255,000 drachma, and I borrowed 150,000 from the Post Bank, to be paid off over twenty-five years at an annual interest rate of six and a half percent.

Athens, June 1972

D. Kallifatides

I am sitting on the balcony of that very apartment thirty-three years later, with his narrative on my lap while my mother prepares lunch. My father left her as a "princess," as she says herself. She owns her apartment, and it makes her happy every time she thinks about it.

It is an old building, but very well constructed and with excellent acoustics. If you cough, you wake the neighbor. My mother lives four floors up from the street. The balcony is her place of refuge. She takes care of her plants and flowers. My father did the same. My mother sits there as often as the weather allows. She doesn't really need to be doing something. She is content to sit and simply gaze over toward the Acropolis, which can sometimes be seen, or toward the mountains surrounding the city. She sits there and thinks about everything that has passed.

I have inherited the same gift or disorder. Sometimes I allow life to live with me, instead of vice versa.

So now the manuscript is done. So am I. A feeling of emptiness leaves me sitting motionless, without even lighting my pipe.

It is the absence of my father, spreading through my chest. I wait patiently until it reaches my throat.

Then I will begin to talk.

We mustn't give up.

LUNCH IS A LITTLE sad, thanks to my impending departure. My mother tries to be brave, entertaining me with stories from the time when I was too young to remember them. For example, the day I pushed my whole hand into a beehive. A neighbor saw me and came rushing to rescue me, but the bees didn't sting me.

"That was strange. I usually get stung by everything that flies, if it doesn't end up in my eyes."

"I'm the same," my mother says, offering an explanation. "We are simply 'sweet-blooded.' That's why the girls like you. When you were little they used to fight over who was going to look after you. They would take you to the water pump and bathe you when it was hot."

I like that explanation. For once it also speaks to me. I have a memory of young girls, passing me from one to the other. I was maybe three years old. It was summer. Hot.

I was completely naked and I had an erection. The girls laughed and fiddled with me.

It can't be helped. There is something ridiculous about a man who suddenly gets an erection. Imagine if it were our noses that grew instead? That would be even more ridiculous—excited men with enormous noses, running around the streets and squares! I begin to laugh at my fantasies, which makes my mother ask what I am thinking about. Of course I can't tell her, so I come up with a couple of stories about things my grandchildren have done and said.

"If only they were here so I could hold them in my arms."

"Mom, whatever we do there is always someone missing," I say with a certain sharpness to my tone, because I feel her comment is a covert criticism of me, because I had chosen to leave.

She realizes she has hurt me, so she changes direction.

"Are they like you?"

"They're both curious."

"What is this and what does it do?"

Once again she is imitating my favorite question when I was a little boy. She tries to smile, but I can see she has tears in her eyes.

I can't pretend that I haven't noticed them.

"Mom, we'll soon see each other again."

IN THE AFTERNOON I go for a long walk around the district. It isn't a dramatic leave-taking, more an attempt to be a young boy again for a while, with his whole life ahead of him.

It is successful, mainly thanks to a group of children from several different countries who are playing football. One of them kicks the ball straight at my head.

"Sorry, that wasn't meant to happen!" says the skinny Black girl who was responsible. I guess she is from Eritrea. In a few years her beauty will be capable of stopping traffic.

"On the contrary," I reply. "It was definitely meant to happen."

She looks at me without understanding.

I sit down at the roughest café on the square, order yogurt with honey, and I am fifteen years old again.

I have my whole life ahead of me.

We always have our whole life ahead of us. At least the part that remains.

I wonder how my life would have turned out if I hadn't left my country. If I had stayed near this square and grown old along with it. But then I wouldn't have had the life I've actually had. Suddenly I feel so ungrateful and so deeply disloyal to all those who have crossed my path, and most of all to my wife and children.

I realize: *I no longer have the right to wonder what another life might have been like. My life is the way it is.*

This simple thought gives me such great relief, almost happiness. I am finally free of man's—and particularly the emigrant's—greatest fear: of having lost your life. I haven't lost my life. I have found it.

My mother is right. It is not the thorns on the rosebush that are the miracle—it is the roses.

———

WHEN I GET BACK to the apartment, a huge problem has been solved: what to send to the great-grandchildren. My mother takes out her wallet, removes two fifty-euro notes.

"One for Cassandra and one for the boy."

She finds it difficult to say Jonathan. My father had problems saying Gunilla, my wife's name. And I had an issue with pronouncing the letter *r* when I was little.

But before handing the notes to me, she rubs them over the top of her head.

That is the blessing. Let these two notes multiply and become as abundant as the hairs she has left on her head, and there are many.

Then it is my turn. I take out a euro note and give it to her.

"I don't need anything, my son."

"It's only for luck, Mom. And for your blessing."

She rubs that note over her head too.

Blessings upon you
Now and for always
From the bottom of my heart
In joy and pain,

she intones, and I can't resist teasing her.

"It doesn't even rhyme, Mom."

She isn't going to let me win.

"You're the writer."

I was never going to get the last word.

SHORTLY AFTERWARD MY BROTHER and his family arrive to say goodbye. My sister-in-law has brought a small gift for my wife. My brother has bought two pounds of feta from someone he knows. I start to get anxious. What if they open my suitcase at Arlanda?

However, I dare not protest.

We have a couple of whiskeys. My mother and my sister-in-law take the opportunity to have a cigarette under my protection. My brother has given up smoking and claims that he has developed an allergy to smoke. My nephew has just read my book and liked it. I am pleased. He is an intelligent young man, a theoretical physicist.

"And soon it will be the football World Cup," my brother says.

Things just couldn't get any better.

He will pick me up the next morning at precisely ten o'clock.

When they have gone, I start packing.

As well as the box of kourambiedes, my mother also wants to give me a smaller box of kadaifi, a kind of honey cake that she claims my wife is especially fond of. In order to make room for all these gifts, I have to leave my slippers behind.

"That's fine—they'll be waiting for you next time you come," my mother says with satisfaction.

THAT NIGHT I LIE on my sofa bed and think about how much of what we say and do are rituals that have been there from the start—but some are not.

My mother's story of how afraid everyone was of "the hole" has made the deepest impression on me. The inherited fear of the bottomless abyss has followed man ever since the beginning of time. The danger of being thrown off the earth, as one is thrown off a bolting horse. The loss of Paradise is also regarded as a fall.

Somewhere in the mountains around my village was the gateway to the underworld through which Dionysus, the god of drunkenness and lust, came up to join human beings once a year.

For several thousand years we have been afraid of the depths. There have always been bottomless seas, lakes, holes in the ground. It was only a few decades ago that we also became afraid of heights. From being afraid of falling off the earth, we are now also afraid of falling to the earth from a height.

Should we count this as a success?

Perhaps. But basically it is the same narrative: the great fall.

IN THE MORNING WE do everything we can to avoid looking at the suitcase.

"Give everyone a hug from me," my mother says. "And you need to start taking care of yourself. You're as skinny as a goat. The years are passing. You're not a teenager anymore."

"And what about you?"

"I'm too old. I can't get any older."

It is a staggering argument, but maybe not so dumb. "I'm so old that I can't get any older." I must remember that. I have a book to write. Another gift from her.

"What is said in the home should not be repeated in the square," the ancient Greeks used to say. I was prepared to honor that rule, but in fact I had always written about myself, about my family, and about others who have been close to me. However, I have never wanted to expose anyone.

There is a popular view that a person's secrets provide a truer description of him or her. This is largely incorrect.

Describing the cellar of a house does not provide the truest description of the house.

People are registered, monitored, taxed, exploited, measured, manipulated, deceived, tricked, cowed, imprisoned, tortured, killed. That's not enough. They have to be *exposed* as well. To hell with that. Who is going to love them? If artists and authors start playing judge and jury who will be left to kiss people's wounds? Who will transform these wounds into flowers?

My parents lived through many difficult times. They might have done things they weren't proud of. They might have had secrets.

I am not interested in these secrets, I am not an undercover cop.

A single light in the darkness is enough for me.

My father was such a light, and my mother still is.

The cost of the light is the shadows it creates.

"We'll see if I get to read that book," my mother says.

"We said you're going to live to be a hundred."

I pick up my case, press the button for the elevator. I give her a hug.

"Go in peace, my child."

She has a smile on her lips and tears in her eyes. She is leaning on her stick, stooping slightly.

I put down my suitcase, hug her again. She smells exactly the way she always has. Of lemons.

MY BROTHER IS PUNCTUAL. I am a little sad.

"This is the first time she hasn't come down," he says.

On every previous occasion my mother has accompanied me all the way out into the street. Not this time. She is wrong. She isn't too old to get older.

I am sad, but at the same time I long to go home. To my family, my friends, my study with its view to the north of St. Catherine's church with its shiny new dome.

We are quiet in the car. It is Sunday morning. Hardly any traffic. The highway ahead of us is virtually empty. The sky above us is completely empty.

"We're so lucky to have her," my brother says.

It is just as true as the last time he had said it, and on her balcony I had found a sentence that I am not going to write down now. It is not the end of this book, but the beginning of the next.

That is what it means to have a mother. You always carry a beginning with you.

Bungenäs, August 6, 2006

AFTERWORD

THE HAMBURG SYMPHONIES WERE composed by Carl Philipp Emanuel Bach (1714–1788), and date from 1733. I was captivated by them the very first time I heard them, particularly as they were written by someone who was a son to an even greater degree than me. Carl Philipp's father was Johann Sebastian Bach, the man with a divine lust—he had a horde of children—and a lust for the divine; no one has come closer to God through music.

I wrote this book with those symphonies on my CD player. I put on that music and that music alone as soon as I sat down at the computer, and also when I didn't want to sit down at the computer.

I am convinced that it would have been a different book without that music, or perhaps it wouldn't have been written at all.

So thank you, Carl Philipp Emanuel, from one son to another.

Finally I would like to dedicate this book to my grandchildren Cassandra and Jonathan—and to my future grandchildren, just to be on the safe side.